ANGELS UNLIMITED

WINGING IT

Annie Dalton

Galaxy

CHIVERS PRESS
BATH

First published in 2001
by
Collins
This Large Print edition published by
BBC Audiobooks Ltd.
by arrangement with
HarperCollins Publishers Ltd
2003

ISBN 0 7540 7866 3

British Library Cataloguing in Publication Data

Dalton, Annie
  Winging it.—Large print ed. (Angels unlimited)
  1. Angels—Juvenile fiction 2. Fantasy fiction
  3. Children's stories 4. Large type books
  I. Title
  823. 9'14[J]

ISBN 0-7540-7866-3

Printed and bound in Great Britain by
Antony Rowe Ltd., Chippenham, Wiltshire

*With love to my three favourite angels,
Anna, Reuben (the original
DJ Sweet Pea) and Maria, whose
sparklingly fresh ideas and stern
criticism brought Mel and her angel
mates to life.*

CHAPTER ONE

I hadn't exactly planned on becoming an angel. But then I hadn't planned on dying young either. Well, you don't, do you?

If I'd thought about it, I'd have said that kind of thing was strictly for Venetia Rossetti. Venetia was a big hit with all the teachers at my school and WAY more suitable angel material than yours truly.

But there you go. Venetia's still on Planet Earth, writing her little poems about rain and violets. And I'm, well—not!

Know what I thought, when I got knocked down?

Now I'll never get the chance to prove

 1

Miss Rowntree wrong!

See what I mean? My last moments on Earth and that's all I could come up with. I am SO not poetic.

I wouldn't want you to get the idea I was a totally bad person. I didn't torture small animals, or go raving about our estate, scaring old ladies. I just couldn't get psyched up about school stuff, like exams or team games, or figuring out what I was going to do when I grew up (though as it turns out, I didn't really need to worry about that).

Shortly before I died, Miss Rowntree caught me flipping through a magazine in class. Honestly, you'd think I'd committed a major crime! 'When will you realise there is more to life than makeovers, Melanie?' she yelled.

But I do, Miss Rowntree, I do, I thought. There's watching MTV. Hanging out with my mates. Ooh, and flirting with boys. And most sacred of all, yahoo! SHOPPING!

But I didn't share these thoughts with my teacher. I might be a bimbo but I'm a very *polite* bimbo. Whereas

Miss Rowntree showed me no respect whatsoever. 'Melanie Beeby, you are just an airhead with attitude,' she snapped at me another time.

But on the last day of term, she said something so sarcastic, I get the chills just thinking of it.

'School is irrelevant to you, isn't it, Melanie?' she said in a scornful voice. 'You're just killing time until you're spotted by a talent scout and get signed up as a TV presenter.'

I nearly fell off my chair. Did Miss Rowntree have some creepy teacher's ESP? Not even my best friends knew my secret fantasy! It was like she'd deliberately set out to humiliate me, basically telling me in front of the whole class that my sad little daydream would never come true.

I didn't let her see she'd got to me, obviously. I just did my bored shrug, and spent the rest of her lesson peeling varnish off my nails.

But the minute I got home, I bawled my eyes out. First I cried all over Mum. Then Des, my stepdad, came in and I had to choke out my story all over again.

'Silly old battle-axe,' Des said. 'What does she know!'

'Yeah, she's a ole battle-axe,' said my five-year-old sister fiercely.

Actually my teacher is depressingly glamorous. But if my family wanted to picture her as a bitter old bat with bristles on her chin, who was I to disagree?

As it happened, Miss Rowntree's spiteful put-down was the very last thing she said to me, because next day it was the start of the summer holidays.

I'd got an incredibly significant birthday coming up, my thirteenth, so I had some *serious* celebrating to do. My star sign is Cancer and if I say so myself, it fits me like a glove. Shy on the outside, with a squishy caramel centre, that's me.

Sometimes I wonder what I'd have done, if I'd genuinely understood I only had a few precious days left on Earth. Would I have appeared on TV, pleading with world leaders to throw down their weapons and stop all those stupid wars?

But as it turned out, my last days were just enjoyably average. And to be completely honest with you, all I cared about was that I was finally becoming a big bad teenager at last.

The day before my birthday, Des drove me and my two best mates to the local multiplex, to see a cool film with Will Smith in it, followed by a complete pig-out at McDonalds. My actual birthday was purely family, which was nice but slightly boring—you know how it is. Secretly I'd have preferred to fast-forward to the *next* day, when I was meeting up with my mates for a major shopping spree. But finally it was all over for another year.

When I came to bed, my little sister Jade did something really sweet. She sat up in her sleep and said, 'You're my best sister in the whole universe.'

I said, 'I'm your only sister, you nutcase.' And without ever dreaming this was my last night on Earth, I fell into a deep peaceful sleep.

And all the time, like summer birds collecting on telephone wires, angels were gathering around me.

 5

I didn't realise this then, but no-one is allowed to die alone. Ever. Some people see their guardian angels, just before they leave their bodies. I didn't. I didn't see much actually. My last few seconds on Earth went something like this.

One minute I'm crossing the road, humming a tune from a Jewel CD, totally fixated on the stuff I'm going to buy with my birthday money, then—BAM—it's over! Some sad kid in a stolen car snuffed me out. Just like that.

No, I didn't look down and see myself nee-nawing along in the ambulance. And as far as I remember, I didn't whoosh down a long bright tunnel and have a meaningful chat with some guy in robes either. I was just—GONE.

Don't get me wrong. That tunnel stuff could have happened. I could have blanked it out. But here's what I do remember, OK?

I remember a hush which might have gone on for days or hours. I went extremely vague about time at that point. This hush wasn't like normal silence, by the way. You could hear music in it. Far-off music, which throbbed on and on without stopping, like a beautiful humming-top. It was the most blissful sound I'd ever heard.

I totally had to know where it was coming from, so I floated out past glittering stars and planets, passing so close it took my breath away.

Then without any warning, my personal soundtrack was switched back on and—BANG! I was in brilliant sunlight, walking towards a pair of swanky gates with a cool little angel logo on them.

And there, in letters so large and round that even my little sister couldn't mistake them, was the most surprising sign I'd ever seen in my life.

The Angel Academy

CHAPTER TWO

Apparently, when some people arrive on The Other Side, as my Great Nan used to call it, they take one look and go, 'Oh, hello, I must have died and gone to heaven!'

But I was only thirteen. It didn't occur to me I was dead.

What's going on? I panicked. Why am I hanging around outside this snobby school? Big snobby school, to be strictly accurate. Kids of all ages were crowding through the gates.

Hang on, Mel, I thought. This can't be right. It's the summer holidays.

But it didn't *feel* like the holidays. There was a definite first-day-of-term zing in the air. All the kids had that

'Yippee! Can't wait to see my mates!' look about them.

It was like being in a dream. The kind where you forget really vital personal info. For instance, I totally couldn't remember what I'd been doing just before my little trip around the galaxy (which I was rather carefully trying not to think about).

I *could* remember the Jewel song. Also an alarmingly big bang. Perhaps I'd been in some kind of accident, and I was concussed? That would explain why I felt so out of it.

I hung about uneasily as kids streamed past me in their gorgeous designer colours. For some reason, my eyes kept going back to that little logo on the gate. At first it struck me as just your basic logo. Like that Puma symbol, or whatever. Then I realised it was incredibly beautiful. And it wasn't that I *couldn't* stop looking— more like I didn't *want* to.

As I stared, hypnotised, at this dazzling thing, the little angel figure began to grow sharper and brighter . . . and suddenly it was shooting out huge

9

starry rays like a Roman Candle.

I shut my eyes *fast*, telling myself it was purely an optical illusion. And when I opened them again, the logo was safely back to normal. Boy, Melanie, that must have been some bang on the head, I told myself.

I still didn't have a clue what to do. But I was starting to feel pretty stupid, hanging around like a spare part. It can't hurt to have a little peek, I thought. I'll just see what's on the other side of these gates, and if I don't like it, I can come straight back out.

I began to drift casually towards the gates with the others, hoping I didn't look as lost and panicky as I felt.

All the other kids seemed really chilled, kidding about and flirting, which I found quite reassuring. I remember thinking that if I HAD been worried about it being a school for actual angels (which obviously I wasn't), the flirting would definitely have put my mind at rest. Also their clothes, which were totally up to the minute. There wasn't a long white nightie in sight.

10

I *did* notice that everyone's cool fleeces and other stuff had that same little angel logo. Imagine that, Mel, I thought. A designer tag you don't know about!

One of the girls had this big throaty laugh, which started down in her boots. She was a real daddy-long-legs, like me. Everything about her zinged with energy: her springy black hair, her tough-girl walk.

I sneakily attached myself to her, trying to act like I just happened to be going the same way. But on the other side of the gates, I nearly blew my street cred once and for all.

I ought to explain that my old school was pretty much your standard comprehensive hell-hole. But this was practically a *palace*, with gorgeous gardens and domes and spires.

Yeah, but it's still school, I thought darkly.

We were hurrying along a shady walkway. You could see it was really ancient. The stone slabs had actual hollows worn into them by centuries of passing feet. One of my shoes accidentally slipped into a shiny long-ago footprint, and a shiver went through me. It fitted *exactly*.

The girl gave me a funny look. 'Angel vibes,' she said. 'You get used to them.'

But I didn't really register what she said because suddenly I'd got the strangest feeling.

'Do I know you, or something?' I blurted.

The girl froze in her tracks.

Now look what you've done, I scolded myself. She's going to have you down as some needy little groupie.

But she was staring at me with a stunned expression. 'Weird,' she whispered. 'I was just thinking the same thing.' She took a big breath. 'I'm Lola.'

'I'm Melanie,' I whispered back.

Our eyes met for about a split second, and it was like a total replay of my shivery footprint moment. We both quickly looked away again and walked on, side by side.

This is going to sound bizarre, so please don't ask me to explain it. But somewhere inside, I just knew Lola was the friend I'd waited for my whole life.

It wasn't how she looked (although her clothes were lush). It was more like I already knew her really well. And I got the definite feeling she felt the same way. We kept giving each other startled little glances as we hurried along. Like, what is going on?

Melanie, get a grip, I told myself. Do you seriously imagine a girl this cool will want to hang out with you?

By this time, there was so much happening inside my head that I'd split into at least three or four Mels. First, I'm trying not to dwell too closely on what I'm doing here. Second, I've just run into a total stranger who seems like she's my all-time best buddy. Third, we are speeding through these school grounds which are getting more amazing by the minute. And I mean AMAZING! It was all I could do not to squeal like a little kid.

Obviously I still wasn't too impressed to find myself hanging around some strange school in the holidays. But I was starting to see how the right person just might get something out of a set-up like this.

At first, I thought I'd gate-crashed one of those really fogey institutions. The ones that call homework 'prep' and have their own weird little school song on speech days. But parts of the Academy were incredibly futuristic. Plus they had all this water everywhere —trickling along little channels and into pools, bubbling out of fountains. It sounded wonderful, like some kind of dreamy, delicate music.

We even passed a spiral staircase which wound around a real waterfall. I'd never seen anything so lovely as those shining stairs, twisting and turning through crowds of tiny glowing rainbows. It was magic.

But there was no time to admire the scenery. The kids were practically running by this time. We seemed to be heading rapidly for some impressive wooden doors. Carved into them was the same little angel logo I kept seeing everywhere.

And at that point I went into a full-scale panic attack.

 14

If I go in there, something's going to happen, I thought. Something which will change me for ever.

But before I could make a run for it, I was swept helplessly through the doors into a vast sunlit hall.

Inside, the hall was more like a huge theatre, with tiers and tiers of seats. High over our heads was a dome of stained glass. Sunlight poured through the glass, spilling extraordinary colours everywhere.

There was a stage, a very grand one. Right across the back wall was an outsized TV screen, the kind you get at pop concerts, with the words WELCOME BACK in glowing letters.

Teachers roamed up and down the aisles. Their fluttering, deep-dyed robes made them look more like birds than people. This place got more unbelievable every minute! But I couldn't think about that right now, because I'd just registered an extremely unpleasant fact.

There wasn't an empty seat anywhere.

Oh, great start, Melanie, I thought.

 15

Trust you to be the one person left standing in this weird scary hall.

Then I saw Lola waving frantically. She'd actually saved me a place! I squeezed on to the bench beside her. A split second later, a honey-coloured boy in cut-offs slid into the non-existent space beside me. 'You think I'm late,' he whispered, 'but five minutes ago I was surfing.'

Liar, I thought. It was true drops of water were running off his tiny dreads, but he'd probably just washed his hair or something.

Suddenly someone strode to the front of the stage. And without him yelling at us or anything, everyone went quiet.

'Good morning, school,' said the headmaster. 'First, a special welcome to those of you who have just arrived. If you have any problems, don't hesitate to come and talk to me.'

Lola rolled her eyes. 'Yeah, like he's ever here.' Then I think she was worried she'd given me the wrong impression, because she hissed, 'It's not his fault. The Agency takes up practically all Michael's time these days.'

She calls the headmaster Michael! I thought. How hippie-dippie is that!

Michael was nowhere near as imposing as the teachers in their robes. He wore a suit he had apparently slept in, giving the impression he'd just flown in on some long-haul flight. You could tell he was completely shattered.

Then I saw him in close-up, on the TV screen, and had another fit of my mysterious shivers. Michael had the loveliest face I'd ever seen.

It was also totally terrifying.

Of course, it should have been obvious to anyone with a functioning brain cell that this was NOT your average headmaster. But I'd never met an archangel before.

Plus, I can't STAND school assemblies. They make me feel as if I can't breathe. I have to tune them out or I'd scream with boredom.

I caught major yawn-words like 'team work', and even (yikes!) 'responsibility', and carried on scrutinising my split ends. But now and then, a more worrying word caught my attention. Michael used it more than any person I'd ever known. After a while it started getting to me like a dripping tap. Angel tradition. Angel skills. Angel Handbook. Angel angel angel.

Something deeply weird is going on here, Melanie, I told myself. Better check it out. I sneaked a look at Lola. She immediately pulled a silly face.

No way, I thought. Far too normal.

I cautiously scanned the hall. It was true all these kids had an unusual *glow*. But that didn't mean it was a *supernatural*-type glow. Probably their parents made them eat their greens and run around out of doors, you know, constantly.

Just one final itty bitty check. Twisting round in my seat, I gave the kids at the back of the hall a nervous once-over.

Melanie, I know this feels scary, I said to myself, but try to answer truthfully. Do any of these kids look like, erm, angels to you?

I had no idea. What did angels look

like, assuming they didn't come with wings and halos like the one on our Christmas tree?

Oh-oh, I thought in a sudden panic. *They'd look like her!*

Behind me was the most angelic-looking being I'd seen since Venetia Rossetti. She had pale, almost silver-blonde hair, with cute little flowery slides fastened in it, and skin so pure and peachy, it looked totally unused.

The girl caught me staring and nudged the spookily identical boy beside her.

I quickly turned round.

It is! It's an angel school, I thought. That rosy glow isn't vitamins and fresh air. It's heavenly *radiance*!

A terrifying question slid into my head. Why was I hanging out with some bunch of angels? Unless . . .

Somewhere far away, I heard myself squeak with alarm.

100% brain freeze! Did that mean I was an angel too?

Like, did that mean I was . . .

CHAPTER THREE

At this point I had two major headaches.

Headache number 1: I am unexpectedly dead.

Headache number 2: I have accidentally infiltrated an angel school.

There was also a potential third headache which I refused to think about. The idea of me being an actual angel was just a *joke*!

Relax, Mel, I told myself. They mixed you up with one of the real angels on the way over. You'd better tell somebody.

But what will I say? I panicked. I couldn't exactly waltz up to someone and say, 'Erm—anyone reported a missing angel?' I mean, suppose I'd broken some really heavy cosmic law just by being here?

I was in such a state, I completely didn't notice Michael's pep-talk finishing. A woman in purple had started calling out names from a sheet. The hall emptied around me, as kids jumped out of their seats and went to join their teachers.

'Reuben Bird,' said the woman. The skinny boy beside me sprang off the bench and ran down to the front. 'Lola Sanchez.'

'That's me!' cried Lola. A ripple of laughter went through the hall, but Lola didn't seem a bit embarrassed. She went to stand beside Reuben, beaming.

'Flora Devere, Ferdy Devere. Amber Overwood.'

Amber bounded to the front, red-gold plaits whipping madly around her head. The twins sauntered out, like glamorous angel supermodels.

I could feel my palms getting sweaty. Don't say she called my name when I wasn't listening, I prayed.

 21

Hold on, Melanie, I thought suddenly. You're carrying on as if you CHOSE to come here!

I blinked with surprise. So I was. Why was that? It's not like I ever saw the point of normal school. Why in the world would I want to go to some goody-goody Angel Academy? Not to mention that I'm not an angel, I reminded myself.

Then something eerie happened.

The woman with the list looked up and smiled at me as if she'd known I was there all along. 'And finally, Melanie Beeby. Welcome to the Academy, Melanie. We all hope you have a happy and productive time here,' she said.

My knees went to jelly. They'd got my name on their heavenly list!

They actually *believed* I was an angel! You'd think real angels would recognise an undercover human when they saw one. But she seemed totally taken in. When I didn't move from my seat, she gave me another encouraging smile, presumably thinking I had stage fright.

OK, Mel, I thought. Here's your big chance to own up.

'Oops, sorry, Miss. I was miles away,' I muttered. And coward that I am, I floated to the front on my jelly legs.

'I knew it,' Lola burbled. 'The minute I saw you, I KNEW we were going to be in the same class. That's Mr Allbright over there. The guy in the hat. Isn't he a duck?'

With his tufty hair and beaky nose, our teacher did look amazingly like a duck. A sweet, absent-minded little duck. 'Did you have to put that duck idea in my head?' I hissed. 'I'm going to die laughing every time I look at him.'

I knew it was dumb, to try and make Lola like me when I was only passing through. But I couldn't help it somehow.

'I only meant he's cute,' Lola was saying. Then she slid her eyes in Mr Allbright's direction and collapsed in hysterics. 'Omigosh,' she squeaked. 'He really *does* look like a duck!'

By this time, cute Mr Allbright was heading briskly out of the hall. Our class started to follow him. Not knowing what else to do, I followed him too.

'Are you OK?' Lola asked, as we walked across the school campus. 'Because back in the hall, I thought you didn't look OK.'

She looked so concerned, I was tempted to tell her everything. But until I'd worked out what I was going to do about this bizarre angel situation, I couldn't take the risk.

'The thing is,' I said, choosing my words carefully, 'the actual thing is, I can't quite get my head round this angel stuff.' I wasn't exactly lying. But I still felt like a total fraud.

Lola groaned. 'I forgot. You only just got here, poor thing. Did you whizz down a tunnel? I didn't get a sniff of a tunnel. I felt totally cheated.'

'Uh-uh,' I said. 'No tunnel. But I heard some really cosmic sounds.'

'Me too!' cried Amber, her eyes sparkling. 'Isn't it amazing how you don't even feel scared?'

'It is actually,' I agreed. I was quite impressed at myself for being able to talk about my death in such a mature way. Plus, I couldn't help noticing Amber had a tiny blue jewel in the middle of her forehead. I wondered if it was her own personal jewel, or some kind of funky angel accessory, and if so, where you got them.

Don't be silly, Mel, I told myself. You're not staying, remember.

We were passing a stunningly beautiful glass building. Cloud reflections skittered over its walls like playful lambs.

I stared up at the sky. There wasn't a cloud to be seen anywhere.

I gawped back at the building, completely confused. 'How do they DO that?' I breathed.

'I have no idea,' admitted Lola.

'Hey,' said Amber brightly. 'I hope we're all staying in the same dorm!'

I stared at her. 'No-one told me this was *boarding* school?'

Lola gave me a funny little smile. 'Well, you can't exactly go back home at nights, Melanie.'

Amber giggled. 'Ooh, Lola, you're so mean! Poor Mel. She just needs time to adjust.'

I forced a smile. Amber was probably a genuinely sweet person, but I got the feeling that hanging out with her could do some serious damage to a person's tooth enamel.

The class came to a standstill in a beautiful little courtyard, full of tropical plants. Sand and seaweed were scattered around as if left behind by the tide. A salty breeze blew my hair into tangles.

I noticed hammocks strung between the palm trees, their canvas bleached by the sun. Then I gave a squeak of surprise.

'Is that the sea over there?' I whispered to Lola. 'Is that the *beach*?'

This school is something else, I thought. It almost made me wish I was attending the Academy for real, instead of just faking it while I figured out my next move.

'That's the great thing about this city,' Lola was saying.

It had never occurred to me that Heaven might be by the sea. And I'd definitely NEVER imagined cities.

Lola hoisted herself into a hammock. 'It's great to be back,' she said.

Some of the other kids grabbed hammocks too. Flora and Ferdy casually took up advanced yoga poses under a palm tree.

I couldn't believe the way Mr Allbright let everyone mess around like this. Poor lamb, I thought. He's got 'pushover' written all over him.

Our teacher gave me an absent-minded smile. For a nasty moment I thought he'd actually read my mind. Then I decided Mr Allbright was just enjoying some private teacher-type joke.

'Right,' he said, tugging at his ear. 'You'll all be wanting to go and settle into your dormitories, so this is just an introductory session—'

I put up my hand, totally confused. 'Erm,' I said. 'I thought we were going to our form room.'

'You thought right,' said Mr Allbright. 'And as you see, here we are.' He waved his hand at the little courtyard.

Suddenly I knew exactly how Alice felt when she fell down that rabbit hole.

'But this is outdoors!' I said.

'Absolutely,' Mr Allbright agreed warmly. 'I can't stand being cooped up, can you? As I was saying, lessons don't start until the day after tomorrow, so we'll keep this session short and sweet.'

I wasn't going to risk a hammock in case I fell out in front of everyone. So I plonked myself on the sand and sat moodily arranging shells into patterns, while Mr Allbright talked us through our timetable. Yawn yawn yawn, I thought.

Amber nudged me. 'Cheer up,' she whispered. 'After your first term you can choose a special subject.'

Ooh, goody, I thought sarcastically.

Mr Allbright started dishing out book lists. I glanced at mine and nearly fainted. EEK! You're out of your depth here, babe, I thought.

'Oh, before you go,' said Mr Allbright. 'I've been asked to remind everyone about this term's HALO awards.'

He tugged his ear again. 'I'm not a fan of awards in general,' he confessed. 'But the HALO is different. It isn't about individual glory. It's about being a link in a divine chain, a valuable member of a team. I hope that this term I'll see at least one HALO go to someone in this class.'

He started going on about how HALO work had to be done outside school hours (yeah, right!). But I had totally tuned out. One of my least favourite words in the dictionary had to be 'TEAM'. Unlike some people, I was proud to be a unique individual, and I wasn't about to become some boring link in anyone's divine chain, thanks very much! I mean, HALO awards, perleaze!

Twenty-four-hour brainache might be some people's idea of heaven, but it wasn't mine. Get out, Mel, I told myself. Get out now. You are not angel material and angel school is not for you. Just because you've died, doesn't mean people can push you around.

This decision was such a relief, I can't tell you.

Now all I had to do was tell Mr
Allbright.

CHAPTER FOUR

Even as a little kid, I had this ability to wriggle out of tricky situations. Miss Rowntree said I was a natural escape artist. She said every time I'm faced with a situation which I find personally threatening, I slither out of it faster than Houdini in a buttered bikini.

So it took me twenty seconds to figure out how to get out of being an angel. This was my plan. On our first proper day of lessons, I'd make sure Mr Allbright saw me slaving away at my angel science or whatever. By lunchtime I'd be visibly stressing out (pale, sniffing back tears, etcetera).

Then I'd ask if I could speak to him in private. Through choking sobs, I'd tell Mr Allbright I was out of my depth. The Academy was WAY too advanced for a girl like me, and I'd never keep up with the others in a million years. Finally, I'd do that Bambi thing with my eyes and I'd be home and dry. By the time they figured out I was never an angel in the first place, I'd be gone!!

In my mind, I was already off the hook. I don't know about you, but relief makes me really chatty.

'So, what do you guys do after school?' I said.

'Oh, stuff,' said Lola vaguely. 'Shopping.'

Yeah right, I thought. Shopping in Heaven!

Amber's eyes misted over 'Oh, Melanie,' she said. 'I don't even know where to start. You are going to have the best time.'

I took a nice calming breath. OK, so Amber was just a little too sweet. But I could put up with her for forty-eight hours.

'That's all for now, kids,' beamed Mr Allbright. 'I look forward to meeting you again, the day after tomorrow.'

Lola stuck up her hand. 'Sir,' she said. 'Shouldn't you tell us where we're staying this term?'

Our teacher looked astounded. 'Did I forget to do that?'

'Yes, sir!' everyone yelled.

Mr Albright hastily produced yet another list and reeled off names. I couldn't help feeling a happy little buzz when I found out I was staying in Lola's dorm.

Amber looked wistful. 'I'll say goodbye then.'

Everyone started moving off. 'Hope we run into you soon, Melanie!' called one of the girls.

'Very, very soon,' agreed her friend.

They looked as innocent as newborn babes, yet I had the definite feeling they were up to something.

'Ignore them,' said Lola. 'So do you want to go straight to our dorm, or what?'

I'd been dying for the moment when Lola and me could start swapping life stories. And it turned out she felt exactly the same! We drifted towards the dorms, talking our heads off. I got totally overexcited when I discovered Lola was from the twenty-second century!

'That is SO amazing!' I said. 'You were born more than a hundred years after me, but here it's like we're the same age!'

'This place takes getting used to,' Lola agreed. 'People from different times mixed up together. That's why they have a dress code.'

I was stunned. All this groovy gear I'd been seeing everywhere was Angel Academy *uniform*!

'I'll take you into town tomorrow to get yours,' Lola suggested. 'We'll go right after your—er . . .' Her voice trailed off.

'After my what?'

For some reason, Lola had gone really red. 'Who knows!' she giggled. 'Sometimes even I don't know what I'm talking about.'

'Oh, me too,' I said sympathetically. And to show Lola I totally understood, I started chattering on about the time I practically got expelled for lopping six inches off my school skirt.

All at once Amber came dashing back, bubbling with excitement. 'Guess what! I went to sign up for the history club. And it's filling up really fast. So if either of you is interested, you should get down to the library right away.'

'Oh, thanks, Amber,' I said, trying to keep a straight face.

She blushed. 'It's no trouble. I missed some brilliant opportunities when I first got here, just because I didn't know they were available. Anyway, got to go. Bye!' She sped away, plaits bouncing.

Lola grabbed my hand. To my astonishment, she was shaking. 'Mel, is it OK if we check out the dormitory later?'

'Sure,' I said, surprised.

'Come on, the library's back there!' Lola launched herself into an impressive sprint.

I tore after her, totally baffled. Lola couldn't be getting this psyched about some geeky school club, could she?

Apparently she could. 'I'm so glad Amber told us,' she gasped out. 'I am desperate to join this club. I couldn't even get on the waiting list last term.'

'You're really that crazy about history?'

Lola looked amazed. 'Aren't you?'

'I think I'd rather eat my own head,' I said truthfully.

The library turned out to be the magical glass building I'd seen earlier. Instead of rushing in to sign up, Lola dithered outside. 'I won't pressure you if history's not your thing,' she said. 'Wait here if you like.'

I shrugged. 'OK.'

To my surprise Lola looked incredibly fed up. She disappeared through the revolving doors. Next minute she was back, eyes blazing. 'I can't believe it!' she fumed. 'When I saw you, I thought, that girl is my soul buddy.'

'I thought that too,' I said nervously.

Lola stamped her foot. 'Then why aren't you jumping up and down at the idea of travelling through time?'

I gasped. 'They do *time-travel* in this club?'

'Of course,' said Lola. 'Did you think we'd just learn a bunch of dates?'

'Well—yes,' I admitted.

We both burst out laughing. At that moment I made up my mind. 'Erm, Lola,' I stammered. 'I've got to tell you something—'

'Yikes!' shrieked Lola, ruining my big confession. 'Look at that queue! Let's get inside!' She dragged me in through the revolving doors.

There are certain words which make me lose all will to live. 'Sensible' is one. And 'library' is definitely another. But guess what? The Angel Academy library is completely not like that.

For one thing, it has the coolest ceiling. You can actually watch stars and planets performing their amazing celestial manoeuvres.

Lola joined the queue for the history club. I tagged along, telling myself I was just keeping her company. It wasn't that I'd changed my mind about staying.

I got a shock when I saw who was signing us up. If I hadn't known they were angels, I'd have taken them for FBI. Suits, blank expressions—the works. I was positive our guy was getting security-type messages down his ear-piece. But I had a peek and what do you know? There was no ear-piece.

'Who ARE these people?' I hissed.

'Oh, they're from the Agency,' said Lola airily, as if this was obvious.

Before I could follow this up, a boy's voice said, 'Hi, er—Melanie isn't it?'

Do I know any boys in heaven? I wondered, amazed.

Then I turned and saw his face. *Omigosh*, I thought.

You could so totally tell he was an angel. One of those beautiful Italian-type angels you see in old paintings.

'I was meant to meet you at the gate,' he explained. 'But I got held up. You know how it is.'

I managed a dazed nod.

'Still, it looks like you survived,' he said calmly.

Some girls had turned to look at him. They were like sunflowers, turning their heads to follow the sun. I don't know why, but that really annoyed me. Huh, I thought. I bet girls get tongue-tied around him all the time. And with a mighty effort I found my voice.

'Oh, yeah!' I said, in my most unimpressed tone. 'I'm having a great time, thanks.'

'Well, yell if you need anything,' he said, and went back to his friends.

' "Yell if you need anything",' Lola mimicked. 'Except Orlando didn't actually remember to tell you his name! That boy lives on a different planet.'

'Nice eye candy, though,' I said casually.

'Gorgeous, I'd say. He's also the best student the Academy has had since for ever. The Agency sends him on tons of assignments already. Ooh Melanie, just think!' teased Lola. 'If they accept us into the history club, we'll actually be working with him!'

I'll admit this idea did make me go very slightly weak at the knees. Then I mentally replayed what Lola'd just said.

'*Accept* us? You're not saying we have to take a test?'

'No need,' she pointed out. 'They

know everything about us already.'

'That sounds really sinister. You mean the Agency like, runs the school as well?'

Lola sighed. 'It's just common sense. The Agency is in the angel business. Hey, it IS the angel business!' she grinned. 'Though we're supposed to call them agents these days.'

I nodded to show I was keeping up.

'Ultimately, if we get through our training, some of us just MIGHT work for the Agency when we leave,' Lola explained. 'And naturally, the Agency likes to keep an eye on its future employees.'

I'd always imagined angels as just hanging around, being effortlessly holy. I'd never thought of them having to WORK at it. Suddenly I had a worrying thought. 'And these Agency guys can tell if we're, you know, for real?'

Lola laughed. 'Talk about nowhere to run! When they look at you, it's like a total soul-scan!'

'Lola Sanchez?' called a bored voice.

'Totally luminous! They opened

another queue,' shrieked Lola. 'See you outside, Mel!'

This was my cue to make a speedy getaway. But before I could run for it, an Agency official conferred with his invisible ear-piece and beckoned me to the front.

I couldn't believe my bad luck. He must have peeked at my soul when I wasn't looking. Oh-oh, I panicked. I'm going to be exposed as a bogus angel in front of everyone!

'I can explain,' I stuttered. 'There was like, a complete mix-up. And—'

'Ah yes, Melanie,' he said smoothly. 'Perhaps you'd like to tell me why you want to join the school history club?'

And with a terrifying WHOOSH, I was watching myself in flashback—sound, vision, everything.

I was seven years old and a total elf. Mousy hair scraped into bunches, eyes way too big for my face and a pointy little chin. At this point, Mum still dressed me in sweatshirts with cartoon characters on them. But that was OK, because secretly I was a time-traveller.

Whenever I got bored or lonely, I'd

whizz off fearlessly to all the times and places which had the coolest costumes, and have imaginary adventures. Unfortunately, once or twice I made the mistake of shifting into time-travel mode when I was at school. 'Control to Melanie,' my teacher would sneer. 'Feel free to return to Earth at any time.'

Pretty soon I learned that I wasn't time-travelling at all, just daydreaming, which everyone knew was a total waste of time . . .

I came back to the angel library with a jolt.

'Yep,' the Agency guy said into his collar. 'No, you were right, Mike. She's a natural. I'll tell her.' He glanced up. 'Michael says congratulations,' he said. 'We'll be in touch.'

I stumbled out through the revolving doors. Lola was waiting on the steps. Her face lit up. 'You're in! That is SO cool!'

'Lola,' I croaked. 'Did you ever hear of a person who was an angel and didn't even know it?'

She patted my shoulder. 'Come on.

We'll go back to our dorm. It'll be a dump. It always is. But I'll make you some of my special drinking chocolate. What do you say?'

I took a long look at Lola Sanchez, the soul-mate I'd somehow known for ever. And I got the definite feeling my Houdini days were over.

'Sure,' I said, as if she'd asked a different question entirely. 'Why not?'

CHAPTER FIVE

Lola was right. Our dormitory was a total let-down. My room was more like a cupboard. As for the bed, I've seen cosier ironing boards.

Lola's hot chocolate was sinfully delicious, however. It was so frothy it was like drinking through a chocolatey cloud.

'I can't believe you can get this stuff in heaven,' I burbled. 'It has to be about a zillion times more wonderful than the Earth kind.'

Lola pulled a face. 'Actually, Mel, it *is* Earth chocolate. It's my grandmother's secret recipe.'

I grinned. 'That's OK! Where I come from, twenty-second-century hot

chocolate would be considered unbelievably cool! How come you can get it here?'

'Didn't you know?' said Lola. 'We're allowed anything from our own time period which is totally essential to our well-being.'

I felt a little rush of relief. 'You mean like, we can still listen to all our favourite music?'

She giggled. 'Well, I couldn't survive without music, could you?'

'No way,' I agreed happily.

After Lola had gone off to her own cupboard for the night, I stayed up, gazing out of my window at the city lights.

The air in Heaven has this fabulous champagne fizz, giving the impression there's always some wonderful nonstop party going on. But that night, it felt like a party I hadn't been invited to.

I'd never been totally on my own before. Not without the TV nattering in the background. I wasn't sure I'd cope. How would I sleep without Jade's snuffly breathing for company?

Of course, as an angel, I didn't *need*

 45

to sleep at all. We do get tired, incidentally. But it's not like on Earth. It's more like your spiritual batteries run out of juice, if you get me. What Lola calls angel electricity. But like eating and shopping, sleep is a habit I'm in no major hurry to give up. So eventually I washed my face, put on the baggy T-shirt I'd borrowed from Lola and plonked down on my economy-size mattress.

I lay in the dark, telling myself that I had this amazing new life and was not in the least homesick. Then it gradually dawned on me that I could hear something.

It was my cosmic music. Those wonderful sounds which pulled me clear out into space, all the way to the gates of the Angel Academy.

And the longer I lay listening, the less I felt like a tiny ball-bearing in a divine game of pinball, and the more I felt I had truly come home.

I must have gone to sleep, because next thing I knew, someone was having a coughing fit outside my door.

I unpeeled my eyelids. It was still

 46

pitch dark. 'I don't believe this,' I groaned.

'What do you think you're up to, Lola Sanchez!' hissed a voice.

That's Amber, I thought.

'You minx, Lolly!' whispered a third voice. 'You'll ruin everything!'

BAM! My door flew open. Eight or nine girls charged in. As well as Lola and Amber, I recognised Flora and the giggly girls from my class.

'Hey!' I said.

'I'm SO sorry, Mel!' wailed Lola.

'Up you get!' said Flora sweetly.

'Yeah? Going to make me?' I clung grimly to my sheet.

But peachy little Flora was stronger than she looked. She yanked my arm so hard, she totally pulled me out of bed.

'It's an old school tradition!' Lola was saying in a pleading voice. 'It's really not personal.'

'It feels personal to me!' I snarled.

The girls bundled me, kicking and struggling, down several flights of stairs, out into the grey light of dawn. We seemed to be heading for the beach.

'Now what?' I panted, as we scrunched over pebbles and bits of shell. 'Are you going to drown me?'

'Will you relax!' Flora snapped. 'Or we just might have to drop you!'

'Mel, I'm so jealous!' Amber was burbling. 'Didn't you ADORE your initiation ceremony, Lollie? I would SO love to have mine all over again.'

'Be my guest!' I growled.

I noticed that Lola was carefully avoiding my eyes. I got the impression she was totally feeling for me.

About half-way down the seashore, the other trainees dumped me down on the wet sand. We eyed each other uneasily.

'Is that it?' I demanded. 'Can I go back to bed now?'

'No way,' said Flora in a spooky voice. 'It's just begun!'

And they joined hands and began to circle self-consciously around me on the sand, like kids playing 'Jenny is a-weeping'. They were giggling at first. Then they sobered up and started chanting some eerie little rhyme.

At the end of each chorus, they

 48

edged closer, moving me with them further and further down the beach, until everyone was ankle-deep in sea foam. Flora and Amber exchanged meaningful glances. And next minute, those sadistic trainee angels lifted me up and dunked me right down in the sea.

I scrambled up, and tried to wring some of the salt water out of my T-shirt. 'Oh ha ha, how totally hilarious!' I yelled. 'How old are you guys, exactly?'

But my tormentors melted away without a sound. And then I saw why.

There was a golden gleam on the horizon. And walking across the water towards me, out of the sunrise, were crowds of angels.

For a minute I forgot to breathe. The angels paid no more attention to me than a tree would, or a star.

I couldn't help myself. I stepped on to the silky surface of the waves and walked out to meet them. It wasn't weird or anything, like walking on jelly or glass. The sea behaved just the same as always. It was me that had changed.

49

My bare feet splashed and scuffled across the sparkling waters of the ocean, as if I was, well—*paddling*.

I can't sink, I thought. I'm as light as air!

The thought was so incredible I didn't know whether to laugh or cry.

As I drew closer, an angel dipped his finger in the sea.

Omigosh, I thought. I could see clear to the bottom of the ocean, fathoms below. I saw shoals of fish shimmer to and fro beneath us. I saw monster crabs scuttling across the ocean floor, like jagged giant scissors. My angel senses were so acute, I actually saw a baby pearl secretly forming inside its oyster.

A jolt of pure happiness went through me. And for a fleeting moment I understood *everything*.

Then without me moving an inch, I was back on solid ground in my sopping wet T-shirt. And the angels were nowhere to be seen.

Lola was waiting, hugging her knees, still carefully not looking at me. 'I brought you some clothes.'

I took them without a word. I felt totally spaced and peculiar.

Later Lola told me that I was so silent on the way back, she was convinced I hated her! When we reached my door, she stared down at her boots. 'So do you still want to go shopping or what?' she mumbled

I was back to normal in a flash. 'Are you *serious*? We can really go shopping in heaven?'

Lola burst out laughing. 'But first I'm going to buy you the best breakfast you have ever had!'

I was amazed to discover that our school campus was only one tiny part of an incredibly vibey city. 'What's that yummy smell?' I said as we walked into town.

'This is the Ambrosia district,' Lola explained. 'Where all the best cafés are.'

She took me to her favourite hangout, a café called Guru. A bald waiter called Mo brought us the biggest breakfast on the menu.

We stuffed our faces with the most delicious pancakes I have had in my *entire* existence. And while we ate, Lola and I had an excellent heart-to-heart. She told me about her gran, who brought up Lola and her four brothers after their mum died. I told Lola about my Mum and little sister, and how our lives totally cheered up after mum got together with Des.

'I'm scared I'll forget about them,' I said.

'That's not how it works. What changes is, it stops hurting so much.'

There was a short silence. 'So how did you—er . . .?' I asked cautiously.

Lola had a wicked glint in her eye. 'How did I croak?'

'Don't say, if you'd rather not,' I said.

'Hey, it's not a problem, honestly. But it's funny how it's only new kids who ask that,' Lola mused. She cleared her throat. 'If you really want to know, I erm—got in the way of a bullet.'

I gasped. 'Someone *shot* you?'

'Only by mistake,' she sighed. 'It's no biggie, Mel. Trust me, after you've been here a bit longer, none of that stuff will seem nearly so important.'

She grinned. 'You don't fret about losing all those cute little baby teeth now, do you?'

I frowned. 'You're not trying to tell me that being shot is in the same league as losing your milk teeth?'

Lola shrugged. 'There are worse ways to die in my city, I promise you.'

I stared at her. 'But you were just a kid!'

So was I, I thought. And I suddenly felt this lonely little ache inside.

Lola slurped up some of her smoothy. 'It's like this, Mel,' she said. 'Some lives are really long and complicated, OK? They just go on and on, like, like—I don't know, *symphonies* or something.'

I gave her a watery grin. 'We listened to a couple in Music. There was this one that had about a gazillion endings, like durn, durn DURN! And then, blam, blam BLAM! And it *still* wasn't over!'

'Exactly,' she beamed. 'But *our* lives, Mel, yours and mine—they just went flashing by, like songs from a car radio. You know those vibey little tunes that

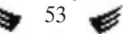 53

put you in a great mood for the rest of the day?'

She hummed a catchy little riff, then broke off. 'Do those songs need to be any longer?' she demanded. 'I don't *think* so, Melanie! They are perfect, just the way they are.'

I couldn't help laughing. Lola certainly had a way of putting things. Though personally I'd have preferred a combo-option. A vibey, feel-good, Melanie Beeby symphony with a gazillion endings.

'You know this morning,' I said, 'when you all rushed into my room? You knew what was going to happen, didn't you?'

'Oh, Mel! I feel so terrible about that!'

'Not the stupid initiation,' I said. 'The angels. Are they . . .?' It was hard to explain what I felt. 'I mean, one day will *we*, like, grow into *them*?'

Lola shook her head. 'The ones you saw perform really specialised cosmic tasks. They deal with the natural world mostly. They don't have much to do with humans or feelings.'

'Or shopping?' I suggested.

Lola giggled. 'OK, OK. I can take a hint, you know!'

On our way out, I was interested to see that Lola didn't actually hand over any money. She just flashed her ID at Mo.

'See you later, Ms Sanchez,' he grinned.

'Hey, do I get one of those?' I asked hopefully.

'Sure, once you get through your probationary term.'

I was horrified. 'You mean the Academy sometimes kicks people out?' Isn't the brain weird? Yesterday I was prepared to tunnel my way out with a teaspoon. Now suddenly I wanted to be voted Heaven's Most Popular Angel!

Lola shrugged. 'You'd have to really screw up to get expelled. Don't look so worried,' she said sympathetically. 'It's never going to happen. And you'll know the instant your probation's up, because that's when you get your like, real angel name. Honestly, that is the coolest moment!' She went all dreamy, remembering.

I felt a pang of jealousy. I wanted to know my angel name too. 'Do you know mine?' I pleaded. 'Can't you tell me? Just a little sneak preview?'

Lola shook her head, still dreamy. 'You're the only one who knows it. It's like something that's already locked inside you. And one day the key turns, and you hear it. And it's like you always knew.'

A vague memory stirred at the back of my mind. 'That's so weird,' I whispered. 'When I was little—'

But Lola had jumped up. 'Come on, Mel! It's time to spend spend spend!'

My mood changed in a flash. 'But I don't have ID!' I wailed. 'How am I going to pay for it?'

Lola's eyes gleamed. 'Melanie Beeby,' she said. 'You are so going to love this place!'

She was right. But several hours later, as Lola and I walked back into Guru with at least a dozen carrier bags, I *still* couldn't believe it.

The instant Lola told the salespeople who I was, they let me have everything I needed. Just like that! OK,

I didn't strictly *need* that sweet little grey dress with all the beading. But after Lola said how great it looked on me, I couldn't bear to leave it behind.

While we waited for our smoothies to arrive, I gazed around Guru, happily admiring the decor. Also, I have to admit, the boys!

Something occurred to me. 'It's lucky everyone speaks such great English here,' I said. 'I am SO useless at languages.'

Lola looked so tickled, that I felt myself turning red. 'What did I say?'

'That's so cute! You really think we're talking in English!' Lola patted my arm. 'Mel, you're an angel! You understand every human language ever invented. But in this city, you speak, well—Angel. Like the rest of us.'

I let my head fall on to the table. 'AAARGH!' I growled. 'This place is too angel for words! Angel this, angel that. Now you're telling me there's some weird angel LANGUAGE?'

'Languages,' Lola corrected. 'If you want to get technical.' She knocked back her smoothie. 'Let's head home

 57

and you can give me an exclusive fashion show.'

'Now *that's* my language,' I said promptly.

*   *   *

We walked home, taking a different route this time. It was getting late and a soft blue twilight was falling on the streets. On the way, we passed this kind of Greek temple building, set in really dreamy gardens. They were like the most beautiful wild flower meadows you could ever imagine, only with that extra heavenly something . . .

Suddenly I stood still. Between the stone pillars, I could see shining beings, quietly moving to and fro. Each of them was surrounded by a haze of coloured light. I was too far away to see what they were doing, but it was so peaceful, it made me want to cry.

'What's this place?' I whispered. 'I mean, is it like some special angel hang-out?'

Lola stared at me. 'Oh, you're good!' she said slowly.

I felt my cheeks getting hot. 'Did I say something stupid again?'

'I'm serious,' she said. 'You really pick up on vibes, don't you? I mean, apart from the Agency building, the Sanctuary has to have the *most* angel vibes in this entire city.'

'But what are they all doing in there?' I asked.

'It's a kind of hospital,' Lola said. 'The guys who work in there specialise in angel healing arts.'

I was just going to ask why in the world angels would need to go to hospital, when quite without warning, a sensation of utter horror flashed through me. It was so strong, I totally doubled up.

Lola shivered. 'They must be bringing some agents back.'

As we stood there, hypnotised, beams of white light came strobing down from the sky. The instant the light-beams touched down, hosts of heavenly paramedic types stepped out. The Sanctuary angels came hurrying to meet them, and both sets of angels started ferrying fleets of gauzy stretchers into the Sanctuary.

From the smooth way they conducted this operation, I got the feeling this was not an unusual event. Everyone really knew the drill. No-one ran. No-one yelled. Everyone was totally calm. Yet there was an electric urgency that you could almost taste.

'If I didn't know this was Heaven, I'd think they'd been airlifted out of a war zone or something,' I whispered.

Lola looked as sick as I felt. 'You'd be right. They just came back from Earth.'

I forced myself to look at the wounded agents being carried past us. It's not easy to describe, but they all had this identical look. Some of them had terrible injuries, but from my new angel perspective, I somehow knew those visible injuries weren't the point. The true damage was deep down. It showed in their eyes and skin, but most of all it showed in their deadly stillness. It was like all their wonderful angel radiance had been drained out of them.

Suddenly Michael was coming

towards us through the crowd.

'Lola, Melanie,' he said quietly. 'You should get back to school.'

One of the Sanctuary staff came out to meet him. They disappeared inside, looking deadly serious.

I realised Orlando was standing next to me. I must have looked like I was in total shock, because he said, 'Are you OK?'

'I don't get it,' I whispered. 'Aren't we immortal now? I mean, how come people can still hurt us like this?'

Looking back, I can see that Orlando really didn't want to be the one to break this to me. His expression was so grim that I started shivering, even before he said the words.

'Those agents weren't hurt by humans, Mel.'

I was bewildered. 'Then who?'

He sighed. 'Their name tends to vary, according to time and place. We generally just call them the Opposition.'

Such a harmless word, but it shook me to the core.

Until that moment, I'd been living

inside some rosy bubble, where angels automatically lived happily and stylishly ever after.

Now the dream was over.

CHAPTER SIX

If there was a dance called the Melanie Beeby, it would go like this. One step forward, two steps back. One step forward, two steps back . . .

It's not that I *forgot* the scene outside the Sanctuary when I got back. It's more that it really scared me. So I told myself I totally didn't need to know about any gruesome old Opposition. It was one of those grown-up things, like the ozone layer, which needn't concern me.

Next day we started school, and I had more important stuff to think about. Mr Allbright might look sweet and fuzzy, but that guy didn't let us get away with a thing.

I know what you're thinking. Melanie Beeby, hitting the books—this is a joke, right? But for your information, I had TOTALLY turned over a new leaf. To be honest, it was mostly down to Mr Allbright. He's a *brilliant* teacher.

In our science class he showed us these cool little atoms grooving away, as if life was one big cosmic party. He said the point of showing us these little guys was so we'd know that absolutely everything in the universe is alive.

'What, even stones?' I said wittily.

'I'm glad you said that, Melanie,' Mr Allbright beamed, and before you could say 'Big-mouth Beeby,' he'd dragged the whole class down to the beach.

'I want each of you to choose a pebble,' he said excitedly. 'And tune into its wavelength.'

Oh, perleaze, I thought. But I had to eat my words. My pebble was SO deep, you have no idea. Luckily stones aren't all that interested in chatting, so Mr Allbright said I totally didn't need to feel bad about ignoring them up until now.

Incidentally, the history club was a complete non-event. Flora and Ferdy were members for one thing. More annoyingly, Orlando didn't turn up. I'd made up my mind to be v. unimpressed the next time I saw him. I'd been practising for DAYS.

Also Lola had completely got it wrong, because time-travel simply didn't come up. All that happened was some guy from the Agency gave us a long lecture about team work (yawn yawn yawn). Then he handed round a humungous book list and said they'd be in touch.

I checked a couple of the books out of the library (Lola made me) but I was too fed up to read them. Well, I never said I was a *total* goody-goody!

I couldn't face the Angel Handbook either, even though Mr Allbright insisted it was essential reading. I got as far as *Chapter 1: FINDING YOUR FEET IN HEAVEN*. Then I came over all dizzy and put it back on the shelf.

That was the day I found out we weren't allowed to take even an occasional sicky. Angels never get sick, apparently. This is very good news obviously. But it made me feel totally trapped. How was a girl supposed to get some rest?

Luckily, according to the, timetable, Wednesday afternoon was our Private Study period. I couldn't wait. Finally, some chill-out time with my best friend, Lola.

But when I knocked on her door, Lola was on her way out.

'Sorry, Boo. I do singing on Wednesdays,' she said. (I have NO idea why she calls me Boo. Lola invents these weird nicknames for everyone.)

'Oh, poor old you,' I said, assuming Lola had been roped in for some kind of holy hymn singing. Then I did a truly noble deed. 'I'll come with you, if you like,' I suggested. 'You know, just this once.'

But Lola explained that Private Study meant you had to go off and do something by yourself. It sounded pointless to me. Why do something by yourself if you can do it with your mates?

I'd hate to give you the wrong idea, though. My new life might be confusing, but it had some excellent moments.

For instance, I'd been dreading the martial arts class. I've always been hopeless at PE. The first session was just a joke. Every time I staggered back on to my feet, another kid knocked me flat.

Just as I was in danger of becoming one big bruise, Mr Allbright told us we were going to work in pairs. I'd been praying I'd get Lola for my partner. So I was not amused when Mr Allbright paired me with Reuben, the kid who was dripping sea-water in assembly, if you remember.

'Why are we putting ourselves through this?' I grumbled. 'I thought angels were supposed to be gentle and holy and stuff.'

Reuben gave an amazed snort of laughter. 'You're kidding! If we let ourselves get too soft, the Opposition would have us totally overrun.'

That chilling word again. I quickly told myself I hadn't heard it.

 67

'They used to teach us to fight with swords, way back,' Reuben explained cheerfully. 'I'm talking thousands and thousands of years ago. But these days the Agency prefers us to learn angel martial arts.'

'And that's another thing,' I growled. 'I don't understand how Time works any more.'

'That's because it doesn't,' said Reuben. 'Cosmic Time isn't something that WORKS. It's something you PLAY with. We play with Time in martial arts constantly.'

I pulled a face. 'Uh-uh, that's way too deep. Translate into bimbo-speak, please!'

Reuben shook his head, grinning. 'I see your little game, Beeby. Ten out of ten for the distraction technique. Now, no more questions, OK? Not until after the class, anyway.'

To my surprise, Reuben turned out to be a wicked martial arts teacher. He didn't mind how often he demonstrated a move. And he never once made me feel stupid. In fact he praised every tiny little improvement, until I almost started to believe I could do this stuff.

Suddenly, to my astonishment, I was flying through the air like a Ninja angel. Wow, I thought, this is so cool. Then I landed on my bum.

Reuben helped me up. 'Isn't this great!' he beamed. 'You're learning to trust those angel vibes.'

'I am?' I said doubtfully. It seemed like a complete accident to me.

'Sure you are,' he said confidently. 'You stopped being scared, and you just flew, right?'

I mentally replayed what had just happened. 'Hey!' I said. 'You're right!'

And for five whole seconds, I was really thrilled with myself.

Then Reuben launched himself into a sequence of gravity-defying moves. Other kids joined in, including Flora and Ferdy. Soon there was this amazing martial arts dance going on. They did some moves in such dreamy slow motion, it really did look as if they'd actually stopped Time.

That's what Reuben meant, I thought.

 69

It was pure magic.

Amber and Lola clapped and whooped with excitement. But all at once I felt unbelievably depressed.

'I'll never be that good,' I sighed.

Reuben flipped himself the right way up. 'Give yourself a chance! Besides, think of all that stuff you do without even thinking. Stuff which is like— impossible for me.'

'Yeah, right,' I said bitterly. 'Just think.'

But Reuben was serious. He was genuinely desperate for help, only he was too embarrassed to ask.

We found out quite by accident a few days later.

Reuben, Lola and me were relaxing near our favourite fountain, when a bunch of nursery-school kids skipped past looking totally angelic.

Then it hit me. They *were* angels. Tiny little angels.

'That's awful!' I gasped. 'They must have died when they were little dots!'

'Uh-uh,' said Reuben. 'Some angels never incarnate. Like me for instance.' He flushed and looked away.

'Erm, is that a bad thing?' I asked cautiously.

'Incarnating is when you put on a human body,' Lola explained. 'It's what you have to do to live on Earth. But little Sweet Pea here never got to make the trip.'

I was amazed. 'You never left Heaven?'

Reuben sighed. 'Don't rub it in. It's been like, my big dream ever since I can remember.'

'I can't believe it,' I said. 'You never even had a *peek* at Earth?'

Reuben looked wistful. 'Not close-up. I've done Angel Watch in practicals.'

'So how come you never went?' I persisted.

'The Agency won't let me,' said Reuben. 'Not until I pass my Earth Skills paper. Unfortunately I just failed retakes. *Again.*'

Quite suddenly I got it. Reuben had to be a totally different kind of angel to me and Lola!

'Lollie, you never told me there were two kinds of angels!' I grumbled.

'There are about a gazillion kinds actually,' said Reuben. 'But yeah, basically they divide into human-angels and angel-angels.'

And in that moment I absolutely KNEW Orlando was an angel-angel. Plus I had deep suspicions about Flora and Ferdy.

'That explains your eyes!' I said.

Reuben looked offended. 'Are you saying I've got weird eyes?'

'Not weird. They're kind of . . .'

'Pure,' suggested Lola wickedly.

Reuben scowled. 'Isn't that another way of saying weird?'

'My sunrise angels weren't weird,' I said. 'Stars aren't weird. Nor is a snowflake, or—a tiny newborn baby.'

'Exactly,' said Lola. 'They're pure!' She grinned at Reuben. 'Like you, my little Sweet Pea!'

'So how does it work, being an angel-angel?' I asked him. 'I mean, did you start out as a tiny cherub and grow up? Or is it that you just look like a typical thirteen year old, but you're actually totally ancient inside?'

'Poor Melanie, that old T-word has

you all confused,' Reuben teased.

'Don't tell me, I know,' I sighed. 'Time doesn't really exist in Heaven, wah wah wah.'

'Oh, it exists! It just behaves totally differently.' He gave a sheepish grin. 'I've never quite got my head around the Earth kind, to be honest. But isn't it something like—there's never ever enough of it to do the things you want to do? And once you make a mistake, that's it. You're stuck with it for ever?'

Lola nodded vigorously.

'I suppose,' I agreed.

'Well, Cosmic Time is different. It isn't this irresistible force you're constantly wrestling with. It's more like this—this never-ending playground, where you can have all the Time you need. You can grow up fast or slow, backtrack a bit, make a few corrections. Whatever!'

'Actually, Cosmic Time IS quite cool,' Lola admitted.

I clutched my head. 'Sorry, this is way too weird for me.'

'Now you know how I feel about Earth Skills,' said Reuben gloomily.

Out of the blue I had this brilliant idea. 'I've got it!' I squeaked. 'You helped me with martial arts, Reubs. Why don't I help you with your Earth Skills? You'll help too, won't you, Lollie?'

I truly thought Reuben was going to burst into tears. 'I can't believe you mean it!' he kept saying. 'I've been feeling like such a loser!'

But by the end of Reuben's first lesson, Lola and I were practically tearing our hair out. It wasn't that Reuben was dim. Actually I think he was some kind of angel genius. He just could not get the hang of the most elementary Earth concepts. Things like bank accounts or bombing foreign countries totally mystified him. 'But what is war *for*?' he kept wailing.

'It's not FOR anything, Sweet Pea,' Lola sighed. 'It just IS.'

'Let's leave war out of it for now,' I suggested. 'I just got some music from home. Let's have a little bop instead.'

Reuben had never heard Earth music before. But he was totally into it.

'They really play this stuff on Earth?'

he said amazed.

'In my time, yeah,' I said. 'In Mum's time—'

'Don't get back on to Time,' Reuben shuddered. 'I'm still recovering from war.'

*　　　*　　　*

What with one thing and another, the days were whizzing by. Mostly I was really happy. Other days I'd find myself missing things from my old life. Silly things, like hitting the late-night garage for emergency M&Ms!

But no matter how good or bad things were, I could NOT figure out what I was meant to be doing on Private Study afternoons.

To begin with, I used it to catch up on those girly chores. Hair, nails, that kind of thing. But I noticed that the others came back, kind of glowing.

The whole thing started to drive me nuts. I felt like the only person in the school who wasn't in on this big secret. Clearly Private Study was not for doing regular school work. It was also not the same as free time. So what WAS it?

Without actually mentioning the mysterious glow-factor, I cunningly quizzed the others about what *they* did.

Reuben practised martial arts. No surprises there. Amber said she played her musical instrument (the harp, presumably). Flora and Ferdy said they did angel mathematics. Yeah, right!

This sounds really sad, but I totally started dreading Wednesdays.

'Everything OK, Melanie?' Mr Allbright asked, finding me brushing tiny grains of sand off the hammocks, as I put off going back to my room for as long as possible.

'Oh, I'm fine, Mr Allbright,' I said brightly. 'Really settling in.'

Somehow I couldn't bring myself to tell a high being like Mr Allbright that I was so shallow I couldn't stand my own company for one measly afternoon a week.

When I got back to the dorm, I decided to wash my hair. It didn't need it. I just wanted to kill some time. But as I flipped the little doodad on the shampoo bottle, Miss Rowntree's voice started up inside my head. 'There's more to life than makeovers, Melanie,' she sneered.

I'm not sure there is, I thought miserably. Not for me.

I was in trouble and I didn't know what to do. 'Help,' I whispered. 'I need help.'

I didn't really think anyone was listening. But they must have been.

Because a few minutes later, help came.

Suddenly, and for no apparent reason, I got this violent urge to go to the beach. It was totally weird. One minute I'm fretting about Private Study, the next my head is full of waves and sea-sounds. It was like this irresistible call.

Yet again I found myself splitting into several Melanies. One is saying, 'What are you ON, Mel?' Another is whispering, 'Come to the seashore, NOW!'

All at once I grabbed my jacket and rushed out.

I stormed along, telling myself I wasn't in jail. I was perfectly free to walk down to the beach if I wanted to.

Sure, if it was actually your *idea*, bird-brain, the regular Mel pointed out.

But once I was sniffing that warm salty breeze, all the Mels magically calmed down.

This was so not like me, you can't imagine! The old Mel *never* did stuff by herself. Yet here I was, walking by the edge of the water, squidging damp sand between my toes.

I've always loved the sea, ever since Mum took me on a day-trip when I was three years old. The instant we got out of the bus, something inside me went, 'YES!'

I loved *everything*. The glitter of light on the waves, the salty breeze, the screams of huge seabirds. And all that SPACE!

Suddenly, the memory that had almost surfaced that morning in Guru came floating into my head.

Mum was holding a shell to my ear, so I could hear the sound of the waves. But I was convinced it whispered my name. 'The shell called you Melanie?'

said Mum. 'Not *that* name,' I kept saying. 'My real name.' But I couldn't explain what I meant.

I smiled to myself, remembering.

Just then some little nursery-school angels came racing across the sand. 'We found you!' they shrieked. They danced me round, giggling. None of them looked any older than four (in Earth years, that is), and they were totally full of beans.

I was bewildered. 'You *found* me? You don't even know me.'

'Yes we do. You're Melanie,' they giggled.

A little boy tugged at my hand. 'Come and play,' he insisted. He had the calmest face I ever saw and absolutely no hair. He looked exactly like a tiny buddha.

'I can't,' I said wistfully. 'I'm supposed to be doing Private Study.'

'Oh, pooh,' said a little girl with a sparkly hairband. 'They just want you to use the Angel Link.'

My heart sank. Kindergarten angels know more than you, Mel, I thought.

'The what?' I said miserably.

'It isn't the Link that matters,' my little buddha explained in a gentle voice. 'It's what happens after that.'

'Yeah, like what?' I said, still depressed at being the slowest learner in Heaven.

His eyes shone. 'You plug into the angel power supply and find your very best self!' he said.

'And you feel all safe and smiley,' said the hairband girl.

'Smiley,' echoed the littlest angel hoarsely.

'It actually makes you glow!' said another little boy.

I couldn't BELIEVE what I was hearing. In two seconds flat, these tots had solved my problem!

'And that's all?' I gasped.

'Not exactly ALL,' he admitted. 'Miss says we'll understand the rest when we're ready.'

'But how do you, you know, plug in?' I asked.

'Oh, that's lemon squeezy,' boasted the sparkly hairband girl. 'Here's what you do, OK? First you get really quiet inside.'

 80

The littlest angel waved her hand. 'Let me, let me!'

'Go on then, Maudie,' everyone sighed.

Maudie took a big breath. 'You let yourself feel all safe and smiley,' she recited in a hoarse little voice. 'Then you picture being the best self you know! And then guess what!' she beamed. 'You ARE it.'

'Miss says when we use the Link, we're connected to every angel that ever was or ever will be,' my little buddha explained.

'Come on,' said the hairband girl impatiently. 'Miss Dove says to bring Melanie back with us.'

The children started tugging me along the beach.

'Miss *said* we'd find you here,' the little buddha beamed.

I stopped in my tracks. 'But how did she know?'

'You asked for help, silly!' whispered the littlest angel.

She clearly saw nothing weird about pre-schoolers picking up someone's personal distress signals. But I was in a

81

total spin.

Melanie Beeby, I scolded myself. Four-year-olds know more than you. You should be ashamed. Go home and read your Handbook from cover to cover.

I didn't, though. Want to know what I did instead? I spent the afternoon in nursery school!

First we did cutting and sticking, involving more glitter than you could possibly imagine. Small angels *adore* anything sparkly, apparently.

Then Miss Dove said we were going to grow tiny orange trees in pots. I thought this sounded almost as boring as normal school. But all the little angels immediately went 'Yay!' like this was some big treat!

'You too, Melanie,' Miss Dove beamed.

'Oh, that's OK, I'll just watch,' I said hastily.

But it turns out no-one EVER just watches in Miss Dove's class. She wouldn't take no for an answer, just briskly handed me my personal tree-growing kit: a little pip and a pot of dirt. And we all solemnly planted and watered them.

At this point, things got a little different to my usual school seed-planting experiments. Miss Dove made us hold our pots in both hands. 'Now I want everyone to go quiet inside and plug into the angel power supply,' she said in her special nursery-teacher voice.

And guess what! With no effort at all, I pictured myself being the best self I could be, like Miss Dove said, and all at once I felt all that cosmic electricity whooshing through me, as if I really was connecting with all the angels in existence.

Next Miss Dove showed us how to beam this energy into our little pots of dirt. 'Gently, gently,' she kept saying. 'We don't want to fry them, children, do we?'

Then we all popped our pots on the window-sill in the sun, and Miss Dove told the children to sing me a new song they'd been learning. I don't know why, but something about their little voices reminded me of those wonderful cosmic sounds which lulled me to sleep every night.

But during the singing, something extraordinary happened. Our orange pips began to put out shiny green shoots! By the time the children had reached the last verse, each pot contained a perfect miniature orange tree!

And I know this sounds silly, but mine seemed to recognise me, because when I picked it up, it instantly burst into sweet-smelling blossom.

I was enchanted. 'I grew a tree!' I burbled. 'That is *so* sublime!'

At last it was time to go home. All the children in Miss Dove's class shrugged on their cool little rucksacks (designed to look exactly like wings), and went racing out of school.

Miss Dove said I'd been *invaluable*, and invited me to pop in any time I was free. I repeated her words to my tiny orange tree, all the way home. 'You were invaluable, Melanie,' I whispered. 'Invaluable.'

The minute I walked into my room, I saw myself in the mirror. And guess what? I finally had that authentic angel glow!

Lola popped her head round my door. She gave me a swift once-over, then grinned. 'I see you finally cracked Private Study then!' she beamed.

'Really?' I breathed.

'Erm, have you checked your post, Boo?' she asked innocently.

I shook my head. 'Uh-uh.'

'Tarraa!' Lola waved an envelope with my name on it. 'We've got tomorrow off! The Agency is having a Dark Study Day. It HAS to be something to do with the history club.'

'Omigosh!' I screamed. *'We're going time-travelling!'*

CHAPTER SEVEN

The minute Lolly went back to her room, I took my little beaded dress out of the wardrobe and tried it on. I told myelf this had nothing to do with impressing Orlando. I just wanted to wear it.

Supposing grey isn't dark enough for Dark Study Day? I panicked. Maybe I should wear black?

Then I had a good look at my reflection. I was looking unusually delicious, if I say so myself. Nah, that's dark enough for anyone, I thought. The dress was a bit on the short side, but so what?

Next morning Lola and I walked downtown to the Agency headquarters.

I was dying of curiosity. I'd been hearing about this mysterious Agency ever since I got here. I couldn't wait to see it for myself.

I'd forgotten that in this city, it wasn't just what something looked like, it was what it *felt* like.

We were still a couple of streets away when a violent tingling started up in the soles of my feet. Then we cut down a side street, and right in front of us was this amazing futuristic skyscraper.

It looked like it was made out of the same magical glass as the Academy library. But instead of a built-in cloud feature, the Agency's tower was continually washed by lovely waves of colour.

In the time it took us to reach the entrance, the building shimmered right through glowing sunrise to twilight lavenders and blues.

The tower was so tall that the upper windows were actually up among the clouds. But through the curly white wisps I glimpsed violent bursts of light. They seemed to occur about a heartbeat apart.

'What's happening up there?' I breathed.

'Oh, the usual comings and goings,' said Lola casually.

My mouth dropped open. 'You mean those are agents like, zooming out of Heaven?'

'Or zooming back again,' said Lola.

I threw my arms around her. 'Totally luminous, Lollie!' I shrieked. 'That's going to be US!'

Amber was waiting for us outside on the steps.

'You look great, Mel,' she beamed. 'Erm, but are you sure you'll be able to run in that sweet little dress?'

I glared at Lola. 'You never said we'd have to *run*!'

'It's a training day, Boo!' Lola grinned. 'I thought you'd work that out for yourself.'

We stared up at the Agency building, working up courage to go in. By this time, its high tingle-factor was making me feel incredibly light-headed. But Lola is not a girl who is easily intimidated.

'OK, we'll do it on three,' she

announced. 'One, two, THREE!'

We dived into the revolving doors and came out, giggling. Unfortunately, the Agency lobby is the size of a cathedral. The tiniest whisper echoes on for ever. The three of us tiptoed across acres of highly polished marble, trying not to laugh, and Lola gave our names to the guy at the desk. Then we stepped into a lift and went whizzing up into the sky for miles.

Now that I was actually inside it, the Agency's whizzy energy levels felt quite normal. But I noticed Lola and Amber had suddenly acquired this extra-special angel glow, so probably I had too.

We hurried along a warren of gleaming corridors, following the signs to the Training Day.

The Dark Study area was crowded with alarmingly advanced angels, all standing around and using angel jargon until I thought I'd scream.

You could just tell none of them would *ever* stoop to taking advice from toddlers.

I was almost relieved to spot Flora

and Ferdy coming through the crowd. A few metres behind them was Orlando.

Just in time I remembered that I had not dressed to impress him, plus I was not one of his sad little groupies. So I gave him my briefest smile and said, 'Oh, hi.'

At that moment Michael came in. I was more clued-up about archangels these days. But I'd noticed that despite Michael's awesome cosmic responsibilities, he never acted as if he was in any way above the rest of us. Sometimes he reminded me of a big brown bear, right down to his podgy tummy. Then I'd see those eyes, blazing with terrifying intelligence, and have to look away.

'Thank you for coming at such short notice,' he said. 'The fact is, we're facing a celestial emergency, and we need all the help we can get.'

I was stunned. This amazing being was actually asking *me* for help!

'As you know, certain eras in human history present the Agency with greater challenges than others,' he went on.

'The Dark Ages is an obvious example.'

I couldn't quite believe this was happening! I'd only been an angel for about five minutes, but here I was at the cosmic hub!

'The greatest drain on our resources, however, comes from the twentieth and twenty-first centuries,' Michael said gravely. 'As some of you will know, we recently received a severe set-back, and a large number of agents were wounded in the field.'

Then he launched into the usual teamwork speech, and how connecting with each other through the Link was normally effortless.

'Unfortunately, on a turbulent planet like Earth, it does take more concentration,' Michael went on. 'Just remember that the principle is the same. Through the Link, you are instantly connected with your heavenly power supply. And the Opposition will have no power over you.'

My eyes accidentally drifted to Orlando, who was sitting down at the front. Pay attention, Mel, I scolded myself. This isn't school assembly. It's real.

'The Opposition naturally prefers humans to believe they are alone in a hostile universe.' Michael took a sip of water. 'It will do its utmost to prevent you carrying out your mission, either by separating you from your team, or by cutting you off from the Link. These Dark Study courses simulate the kind of trouble you can expect.'

We were all divided into teams. All six Academy kids were in one team. Orlando was our team leader.

'Just take a moment to establish the Link,' said Michael.

I sent up a silent thank you to Miss Dove. Thanks to her, I now knew that the Link was some kind of heavenly internet. Luckily, since my afternoon in nursery school, I totally had it down.

I took a big breath, went quiet inside, and WHOOSH! I was connected.

It was effortless, just like Michael said. I felt so peaceful, I knew nothing could ever hurt me again. I could see everyone else felt the same.

Then two agents sprang up from their seats and went to stand on either side of a door. Michael gave them a nod, and one of them pressed a button. The door slid back. When I saw what was on the other side, my mouth went as dry as cotton wool. I'd secretly been hoping for castles and knights in armour. But there was just darkness. Icy cold darkness.

'GO, GO, GO!' chanted the agents, and they began pushing people through the door, one at a time.

Oh-oh, I thought. This is scarier than I thought!

'You'll be OK, Mel,' said Orlando quietly.

I gave him a withering look. I didn't care if Orlando had just read my most private thoughts, I refused to seem impressed.

But at that moment, the agents grabbed my arms and booted me into space.

FLASH! It was a frosty night and I was in a crowded fairground, a disappointingly modern one. Not a bustle or crinoline in sight.

 93

I should explain that Agency simulations faithfully recreate what happens when a celestial agent first hits Planet Earth. Which is basically that it's completely mad.

Suddenly my angelic senses were bombarded with about a gazillion signals.

Can you imagine being forced to listen to all the radios, TVs and stereos in existence? Only Earth isn't just blasting you with a cacophony of *sounds*—it's also broadcasting this nonstop uproar of thoughts and feelings, all rushing through you like light waves. Not only is it scary and overwhelming, it actually *hurts.*

I clutched my head. 'Ow,' I whimpered.

FLASH! Lola appeared beside me. Amber appeared next, then the twins, followed by Orlando.

Ferdy instantly clutched his head. 'Oh-oh! Total brain overload!' he gasped. We were all in genuine agony at that point, but everyone cracked up. It was the most human thing I'd ever seen Ferdy do.

Orlando quickly showed us how to tune most of this hubbub out. You just focus on the Link, and the other stuff fades into the background.

But as it turned out, brain overload wasn't the weirdest thing we had to deal with. Amber gave a muffled shriek. 'Eek!' she shuddered. 'That woman walked right through me! I know she's only a hologram, but it felt SO indecent.'

'Get used to it,' grinned Orlando. 'On Earth, people walk through you constantly.' He cleared his throat. 'Now, we're looking for a kid who's run away from home. Just one problem— the Opposition is after him too. So you're also keeping your eyes skinned for the bad guys. Only, they won't necessarily LOOK like bad guys. They may not look like guys, full stop.'

'So how will we recognise it, erm, them?' asked Amber.

'Practice,' said Orlando tersely.

I gave a mock salute. But secretly I thought Orlando made an excellent team leader.

Actually, the training exercise was

really interesting. We had to run all over the fairground looking for our runaway. We jumped on the dodgems and searched the cars. We hitched a ride on the Ferris wheel. We even went whistling through spooky tunnels on the ghost train.

Unfortunately my dress was totally embarrassing me. I was definitely going to have to rethink my outfit before I went on an actual mission.

Then, like someone throwing a switch, everything changed. You know when the sun goes behind a cloud, how all the light drains out of everything? It was like that. I felt a prickle of horror.

'They're here,' said Orlando softly.

'I can feel it!' I whispered.

'Ugh,' said Amber. 'Slime.'

Lola was deathly white. 'Not slime, treacle,' she muttered in a sleepwalking voice. 'Evil cosmic treacle, oozing everywhere.'

That's when I found out that the Opposition can only be recognised through experience. It's pure evil intelligence which can disguise itself any way it likes. If Orlando had actually explained this, I think I'd have panicked. As it was, all my angel senses were suddenly functioning on red alert. But they were totally focused by this time, so it didn't hurt.

And all at once I heard the boy. Or rather, the boy's thoughts. We all did.

Flora's brow crinkled. 'Melanie,' she said in her clear little voice. 'Does Earth have a thing called a Hot Dog Stall? Because if so, he's there. His name is Curtis and he's nicked his mum's purse.' She frowned. 'I *think* that's what he's saying.'

We all went dashing off to the hot dog stall, and there was Curtis, shivering in a flimsy jacket and hungrily polishing off his frankfurter.

We weren't a minute too soon. Some menacing older kids were heading right for him. In a flash, I saw what was going to happen. Those kids were going to get Curtis into heavy-duty trouble. All because he'd made a stupid mistake.

'Curtis,' I said. 'It's OK. Go home and tell your mum you're sorry and everything will be all right.'

'Yeah, but you'd better clean up your act, boy,' scolded Lola.

'No more *nicking*, young man!' said Flora, shaking her finger.

'Erm, nice try, but use the Link, OK?' suggested Orlando. 'It's more effective.'

We gathered around Curtis so closely that I could smell his hot-dog breath. Then we linked him up with our angelic power supply and *bombed* him with heavenly vibes. Curtis's thoughts calmed down at once. Not only that, the evil treacle phenomenon totally evaporated. It was as if the Opposition simply lost interest. As for those menacing kids, they sailed past Curtis as if he didn't exist.

'They didn't even SEE him,' breathed Amber.

'Well done, team,' said Orlando quietly. He snapped his fingers. 'End program,' he said.

FLASH! We were back in the Training Area.

People were patting Flora on the back.

'What a star,' I told her.

I actually felt quite fond of her. You know, temporarily.

'That hot-dog thing really threw me off,' Ferdy was saying.

But I'd stopped listening. I'd realised something incredibly important.

'Lollie,' I hissed. 'I want to specialise in Time! And when I graduate, I'm going to try out for the Agency.'

'Do you mean it?' Lola gasped.

Was she kidding? From now on, I was going to be the hardest-working, most responsible team member *ever*. Together we'd blaze through time and space on a cosmic crusade. Goodbye, shallow human, I thought deliriously. And hello, wise angel.

But you can't say that kind of stuff aloud, even to your best friend. So I just said, 'Yeah, Lollie, I mean it.'

*　　　*　　　*

Several hours later, we were sprawling on Lola's rug, sipping hot chocolate. 'I'm so happy, it's ridiculous!' I told her.

'Ridiculous is right,' she yawned

'You've got yourself a serious chocolate moustache, Boo.'

It was after midnight. We'd taken part in so many simulations, I'd lost count. We were shattered, but we couldn't quite get up the energy to go to bed. It might sound weird, but outwitting the Opposition in a simulation burns up nearly as much angel electricity as the real thing.

'I wish I'd known this stuff when I was alive,' I said suddenly.

'Stuff?' Lola mumbled.

'Those times I thought I was alone, when all the time the Agency had everything under control. I wish someone had told me.'

'Oh, totally,' said Lola.

'Lollie, there's something I still don't get,' I said.

'Hmmn?' said Lola.

I swallowed. It was like I could hardly bring myself to say the name.

'I haven't got a clue what the Opposition really is,' I confessed.

Lola sat up, frowning. 'Do they have computer viruses in your time, Mel?'

I nodded. 'They're like sinister

 100

virtual life-forms.'

'So why do you think humans fool around with them?'

I ran my finger round my chocolatey mug and licked it thoughtfully.

'I think some people just enjoy committing major sabotage, period.'

'Exactly!' said Lola. 'No-one really knows how the Opposition got into the cosmic system. And frankly, who cares? It's out there now, doing major sabotage. And the Agency can't ease up, or the Opposition would totally get the upper hand.'

'So it's just like—a cosmic glitch. It isn't real, right?' I asked uneasily. I think I just wanted Lola to comfort me. Because deep down, I already knew the answer.

Lola took a long time to reply. Then she said quietly, 'No, it's real, Boo.'

'But the guys in white suits always win in the end, though, don't they?' I pleaded. 'Don't they?'

But Lola silently started getting her stuff ready for school next day.

Suddenly I had to go to bed, before my brain went into total melt-down. I stumbled to my room, and I was asleep before I even hit the pillow.

*   *   *

As a trainee angel, you lead this totally double life. Next day I went to school feeling like the angel equivalent of Buffy the Vampire Slayer, and received a serious shock.

While some of us had been playing thrilling cosmic war games, the rest of the class had started revising for exams.

Remember the words I mentioned? The ones which freak me out? Well for me, EXAMS is right up there with NIGHTMARE.

That night I had my recurring one, where I'm climbing a ladder to the stars and one by one the rungs start breaking off in my hand.

The famous Beeby curse had struck again.

It works like this. The more desperately I want to do well, the more incapable I am of picking up a book. The less work I do, the more desperate I become. As the days went by, I slid into a major depression.

Then one night Lola really told me off.

'You're talking yourself into a corner, Mel. You're not weird, you're not doomed and you're not alone. You've got me and Reuben to help you now.'

Lola's pep-talk broke the spell. She seemed so confident I could do well, I actually believed her. Night after night, Lola, Reuben and I tested each other on all the subjects Mr Allbright had taught us.

When I finally tottered into the examination hall and turned over my first exam paper, I practically fainted. I understood *all* the questions!

After the exams, a gang of us went out to Guru to celebrate. I was still fizzing with relief. 'I don't want to max it or anything,' I told Reuben. 'I just don't want the Academy to chuck me out.'

'I just hope I scrape a pass in Earth Skills, finally,' he sighed.

'Sure you will, Sweet Pea!' grinned Lola. 'And we'll all zoom off to Earth together like the three cosmic musketeers!'

Hours later, I let myself back into my room, and was surprised to hear the chirp of an Agency telephone. Last time I looked, there hadn't been a phone. Yet here it was, beside my bed.

I pressed TALK. 'Erm, Melanie speaking,' I said, feeling extremely silly.

'Congratulations,' said Michael. 'Your Dark Study team did extremely well.'

'Oh, th-thank you,' I stuttered.

'Now let's see how you deal with the real thing. We don't normally send trainees out into the field so soon, but as you know, we've got a crisis on. An Agency limousine will collect you in a few minutes.'

'Oh, where are we going?' I squeaked. 'I mean *when*?' I added hastily.

Michael's voice sounded as calm as always. 'You'll be doing angel duty in the London Blitz,' he said. '1944 to be precise.'

CHAPTER EIGHT

Minutes later I was staring into my wardrobe in deepest despair.

Lola hammered on my door. 'Melanie!' she thundered. 'Get yourself out here!'

'I'm still in my party dress!' I wailed.

'The Londoners won't care if you're wearing a tiara! Most humans can't see angels, remember?'

'You'd better be right,' I muttered.

The limousine picked up Amber and the twins on the way, then sped downtown to Agency Headquarters, where Michael and Orlando were waiting.

You could tell the night staff didn't think a girl in a sparkly mini-dress had

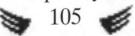

ANY chance in the unending war against cosmic evil. But Orlando didn't seem to notice. That boy is SO on a higher level, it's unbelievable!

I wasn't sure how I felt about spending forty-eight hours with Orlando. Luckily I didn't have time to think about it, because Michael whisked us through Departures at top speed.

Then he handed out angel tags—little platinum discs on lightweight chains. When mine caught the light, I made out a tiny heavenly symbol in 3D.

'These insignia show you're on Agency business,' Michael explained. 'They also strengthen your link with your heavenly home.'

My heavenly home, I thought. This is really happening!

We crowded into the time portal.

'Incidentally,' said Michael casually. 'I thought you'd enjoy going by the scenic route.'

The door slid shut.

'Next stop Earth,' whispered Lola.

Seconds later, the portal lit up like a Christmas tree, and we were catapulted into the slipstream of history.

These are some of the amazing sights we saw. Dinosaurs lumbering around in a steamy dinosaur world. Horsemen in hats with bizarre earflaps, galloping furiously towards a fabulous Eastern city. Egyptian slaves sweating over what would eventually turn out to be the Pyramids.

But my favourite moment has to be when we crowded into an attic in long-ago Italy, where a young man was painting by candlelight.

To my surprise, the room was already bursting with angels, all dressed in gorgeous Renaissance-type clothes—except for the cherubs, who just wore tiny wisps of gauze. The angels all had soulful eyes and dark curly hair, like Orlando. They murmured politely as we came in, then went back to zapping the artist with inspirational-type vibes.

'That's Leonardo!' said Orlando.

Lola gasped. 'The da Vinci guy?'

Orlando nodded. 'He's a major Agency project.'

I edged up to Lola. 'How come

there's all these like, old-fashioned angels here?'

'Sometimes Earth angels get posted back to their own time period,' she whispered. 'To help out with some special mission.'

'It feels just like home,' breathed Flora.

It was true. Leonardo's attic room had the *most* angel electricity flying around. I suppose that's how he managed to stay awake all night, creating masterpieces, while everyone else in Italy just snored their heads off.

Then we were away again, whirling through history like divine dandelion seeds.

This time I got the definite sense that some historical periods were, well—DARKER than the rest. Suddenly it dawned on me that these parts just might have something to do with the Opposition. Then I wished I hadn't had this particular thought. Because minutes later we arrived in wartime London, and there was no light anywhere.

I know it doesn't sound very angelic,

 108

but I felt a moment of pure panic. The place looked totally empty. Then I saw dozens of feeble little torches bobbing along in the dark.

Lola froze beside me. 'Why is everyone creeping about like spies?' she whispered.

'It's the blackout,' I hissed. 'People aren't allowed to show lights.'

'So what's all that luminous spaghetti up there?' she said. Shafts of white light were criss-crossing the rooftops.

'Searchlights,' I told her.

Amber looked impressed. 'Boy, you've really been reading up on this.'

'Not really. We did it in History,' I whispered. 'Plus I must have seen about a gazillion war films on TV.'

It's not often I get the chance to show off my superior knowledge, right? Maybe I should have milked it a little longer. But I was in shock.

I totally didn't recognise this depressing city, with all these jagged spaces where houses ought to be. At night-time, *my* London blazed with every kind of light. Car headlamps, street lights, neon signs. This London was too dark and dismal for words.

There was a bomb crater right in the middle of the street. But the local Londoners just calmly walked around it, like it was no big deal.

There was a sickly smell of leaking gas, plus a smell of burning like you wouldn't believe.

We'd landed outside a pub called the Angel. I think that was probably Michael's little joke. Inside, people were having a singsong, belting out that really cheesy one about bluebirds and the cliffs of Dover.

Flora winced. 'They're in tremendously good spirits,' she said bravely.

Suddenly an eerie wailing filled the air, wavering up and down the scale. My tummy looped the loop. Oh-oh, I thought, that's the air-raid warning.

'We'd better get going,' said Orlando.

We joined the crowds streaming into the Underground. It was really uncomfortable. People barged right through me as if I was thin air. I told myself it wasn't personal. I'd probably walked through a few angels myself in my time.

But when we reached the platform, I almost bolted straight back up to the street. Practically the entire neighbourhood had come to spend the night in the tube. The air stank of underground trains and stale smoke, plus that sour pong of people who could use a really good shower. Friends, relations and total strangers all squashed together like factory chickens, cracking jokes and eating sandwiches, even knitting, as calmly as if they were in their own living rooms.

The younger children were mostly tucked up, fast asleep, unaware of the planes droning overhead. Except one tiny kid who couldn't stop coughing. His cheeks were hot and red and he was getting really upset.

'Hey, small fry!' Lola said softly. 'Would you like me to fix that mean old cough?'

The little boy's eyes opened wide. He stretched out his arms, smiling.

'He can see her!' I breathed.

'Of course he can!' said Orlando.

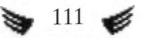

'Toddlers are much smarter than grown-ups.'

There was a huge explosion overhead. I squeaked with fright.

'Don't tell me the Agency's sending babies now!' said a clipped British voice. 'Enjoying the pretty fireworks, darlings?'

Orlando grinned. 'Hiya Celia! How's it going?'

And suddenly I saw that the tube station was full of Earth angels, all wearing elegant 1940s clothes. They waved briskly, then went back to work.

'Splendidly, thanks,' Celia was saying. 'Luckily you've come on a quiet night. Absolutely no sign of You Know Who.'

And she and Orlando launched into one of those advanced angel conversations which I totally couldn't follow.

'So what are we supposed to do, exactly?' I asked Amber.

She looked surprised. 'Just be yourself, of course.'

But Celia's glamorous army made me feel totally inadequate. I felt like some sad girl who was just *pretending* to be an angel. I looked around for Lola but she was still cooing to her toddler.

I can't do this, I panicked. I shouldn't have come.

Then I saw Molly.

She couldn't have been more than six years old, but she had the wisest eyes I've ever seen on a human being. The other kids were all in big family groups. Molly was just with her mother. Her mum was really young and full of beans, more like a big sister really— kidding around and pulling her daughter's pixie hood over her eyes.

'I want you to tell me a story,' Molly kept saying.

'Slave driver,' sighed her mum. She put on a posh voice. 'All right, which story does Modom require?'

Molly's mum was a wicked storyteller. Her version of *The Princess and the Pea* was a hoot.

And with a brilliant flash of inspiration, I saw how I could make myself useful. I crept up really close to Molly and her mum, linked myself up with my power supply and began radiating lovely vibes.

Other kids began to edge closer. Soon Molly's mum had this crowd of spellbound children lapping up every word. I decided I could get seriously hooked on being an angel. Between us, we'd created this charmed circle, and now everyone was desperate to be inside it.

All at once, there was another massive explosion. You could see people shudder, wondering if it was their street, their house, which had caught the blast. But without missing a beat, Molly's mum carried right on describing how the old queen made up the bed with twenty quilts and twenty feather beds. And she kept going until she reached the part where everyone got to live happily ever after.

'Go on, missus,' said one of the older kids wistfully. 'Tell us another.'

Ahhh, this is SO sweet, I thought. Then I almost jumped out of my skin. Scary Celia was standing next to me!

'Well done, dear,' she said. 'When humans and divine personnel work together, that's when miracles happen!'

I looked round to see who she was talking to. But she meant *me*!

'Keep up the good work!' said Celia. And she whisked away down the platform to terrify someone else.

CHAPTER NINE

That night our shelter absolutely rocked! But at last the enemy planes went droning away towards the English Channel and everyone could get some sleep.

Before daybreak, I glanced up and saw Orlando watching over a sleeping soldier.

'Poor guy just came back to find his house a pile of rubble,' he said. 'No-one can tell him where his family's gone.'

The man's eyelids began to flicker, and his exhausted face took on a strangely peaceful expression.

'He's dreaming,' I said softly.

'He used to be a gardener,' Orlando

sighed. 'Before he went off to fight. I thought he could use a restful garden dream.'

'You can send dreams?' I breathed.

He gave me one of his heartmelting smiles. 'It's no big deal. I'll teach you some time—if you're interested,' he added shyly.

Neither of us spoke after that, but it wasn't an awkward silence. Actually, it was lovely.

Shortly after dawn, people began to stir, gathering up babies and belongings.

'Button your coat, Moll,' her mum grumbled. 'I've got to be at work in half an hour.'

'My fingers won't wake up,' Molly complained.

I felt really sad as they hurried away. I'd watched over them all night. Now I knew their hopes and fears as well as my own. I know that tuning into human thoughts must sound like some major celestial ability. But the fact is, once you're an angel it's impossible not to. They just jump out at you like radio waves.

117

That's how I knew that Molly's dad had been killed in action, less than six months ago. Now they were all alone.

By a strange coincidence, I'd lost *my* dad when I was Molly's age. He didn't die though, he left. And I know this is corny, but for ages after that, I was terrified Mum would leave too. One time she was late picking me up from school, and it was like my whole world totally crumbled. So I had a pretty good idea what Molly was going through.

Lola nudged me. 'Control to Melanie,' she teased.

I blinked. Celia wafted up. 'I probably won't need you chaps until tonight,' she said. 'Why not make yourselves useful upstairs?'

'Excellent,' crowed Lola. 'We can be time-tourists!'

We emerged into a November dawn. It was wonderful to breathe the damp London air after our long night underground.

'Omigosh,' said Amber suddenly.

A family were eating breakfast in their living room. Dad in his collar and tie, Mum in her apron, plus three little kids, all politely sipping tea and passing the toast and marge. It was like a scene from a picture book. Except for one thing. The front had been blown clean off their house.

And I remembered Reuben saying, 'But what's war *for*?'

Lola had both hands pressed tightly to her mouth. 'Whatever kind of bomb does that?' she whispered.

'The Germans have started sending over these weird buzz bombs,' Ferdy explained earnestly. 'They're like aircraft, except they don't have pilots. They just point them in the right direction, then when they arrive— BOOM!'

'My Great Nan called them doodlebugs,' I said. 'She said the first time one came over their house, she almost wet herself.' I had a sudden thought. 'Ferdy,' I said, 'how come *you* know so much stuff about 1944?'

When Ferdy tosses his hair about, it means he's going to say something wildly superior. 'Don't you ever use the Link?'

'Me?' I bluffed. 'Never! I prefer to like, improvise.'

'Boo, you are so-o bad!' giggled Lola.

Everywhere, we saw constant reminders of the war. Queues outside food shops, sticky tape over the windows, sandbags in doorways. But instead of letting themselves be crushed, people just sprang up again like daisies, totally surprising you.

I don't want you to think we were *just* being time-tourists. Lola and I spent hours with a really good-looking fireman, while his mates dug him out from under a pile of rubble.

He was more of a fire*boy* really. His name was Stan and he'd been searching a bombed house for survivors when the roof fell in. He was in a lot of pain, but he kept up a stream of daft jokes.

Finally the firemen lifted him free. As the ambulance doors closed, we heard Stan yell, 'Tell those two pretty girls to wait for me, do you hear?'

'Poor Stan,' muttered one of his mates. 'He's really concussed.'

I jumped up, tugging down my dress as far as it would go.

'This is your fault, Lollie,' I blazed. 'I can't believe I've been sitting here in this little dress and Stan the fireman could SEE me!'

Then we heard a low growl in the distance.

'Erm, I think that's a buzz bomb,' I said.

'One flying bomb's not so bad,' said Amber brightly.

Ferdy was looking unusually nervous. 'Actually, they send them in relays.'

People were already hurrying for the nearest shelter.

The siren began its stomach-churning wail.

As the bomb came nearer, the air was literally juddering with vibration, as if it was compressing itself into some terrifying new element. I think Orlando saw how scared I was, because he suddenly grabbed my hand.

'We'll do this the easy way,' he yelled. 'Touch your angel tags and focus on the shelter. On a count of three. One, two—three!'

I obediently shut my eyes and FLASH! We were underground, as everyone came fleeing down from the street.

BOOM! The first buzz bomb exploded overhead.

Celia appeared, looking wonderfully chic. 'Chaos, isn't it?' she said. 'Let's see what we can do for the poor dears, shall we?'

We started beaming angel vibes at the traumatised Londoners.

I realised Orlando was standing really close to me. I tried not to dwell on the fact that he'd recently held my hand.

'How did you do that cool fast-forward trick?' I murmured.

Orlando sighed. 'Mel, you really ought to read your Handbook!'

We went back to work. It probably sounds terribly hippie-dippie, but transmitting angelic vibes in a crisis is actually just common sense. Negative emotions make it that much easier for the Opposition to home in.

But for some reason I kept looking up every time someone came down into the shelter. The stream of arrivals slowed to a trickle. As the third buzz bomb exploded overhead, I realised what was bothering me.

Molly and her mum weren't there.

In an instant of total clarity, I knew Molly was in danger. I've got to go to her, I thought.

But Orlando completely put his foot down. 'You know the score, Mel,' he said firmly. 'No heroes, no stars. Just links in a divine chain. Those are the rules.'

I took a deep breath, trying to stay calm. 'I'm not trying to big myself up, I swear. But Molly's only six and she's all alone in an air raid. I *saw* her. Orlando, it's like I'm meant to save her or something. It's—it's—' I searched desperately for the right words. 'A genuine cosmic emergency!'

But Orlando was not remotely impressed. 'Remember that time outside the Sanctuary? Those agents had a cosmic emergency too. And the Opposition picked them all off like apples.'

I really lost my temper then. 'Well,

EXCUSE me,' I yelled. 'But I think a little girl is more important than some old rule!'

'Boo,' Lola whispered. 'Everyone's looking.'

Celia's angels were staring in horror. It was like being back at school, only about a billion times worse. Plus now even my best friend was against me.

'I know it must seem harsh,' said Orlando quietly.

'Not harsh,' I said through gritted teeth. 'Inhuman.'

Orlando's calm expression didn't flicker. 'Just get on with your work, Mel, OK?'

I stared at him. Couldn't he see that Molly and her mother *were* my work? Obviously I'd have to take care of this all by myself.

I sneaked a last yearning look at Orlando. Get real, Mel, I told myself. A gorgeous genius and an airhead with attitude? It was never going to happen!

I didn't try to hide what I was doing. In front of everybody, I touched my angel insignia, and focused on Molly with all my heart.

FLASH! I was outside a terrace of tall thin houses in the fading light.

A weird-looking aircraft hovered at rooftop level. Angry flames jetted out of its ugly backside. A distinctive buzz-bomb growl filled the air. Then it stopped and there was a deathly hush.

The buzz bomb dropped behind the terrace like a stone. Then BOOM! The whole world came crashing down. Jagged shards of glass, clouds of brick dust, actual bricks, half a chimney pot.

Out of instinct I dived into a doorway.

'You're an immortal being,' I reminded myself. 'Get a grip.'

At that moment I heard a scared whimper. 'Mum? Where are you, Mum?'

I scanned the street, until I saw a basement door swinging on its hinges. 'Hold on Molly!' I called ridiculously, though I knew she couldn't hear me. 'I'm coming.'

I found her crouching under the kitchen table, whispering the same words over and over. 'Come home, Mum,' she was whispering. 'Please don't be dead, Mum. I'll make you a cup of tea just how you like it. Please don't be dead, Mum.'

I couldn't bear it. I completely forgot I was an angel.

'You don't have to be scared. I'm here now,' I said softly.

But as I reached for her, I caught a stealthy flicker of movement in the hall. Just the tiniest flicker. And suddenly it was impossible to breathe.

Then I heard a voice so intimate, I seemed to have known it for ever.

'Hi Molly,' it said. 'I've come to take you down to the shelter.'

The tiny hairs rose on my neck.

A boy was lounging in the doorway. He wasn't looking at Molly. He wasn't looking at anything. He was just *there*, smiling at some private joke.

He had bleached blond hair and the bluest eyes I've ever seen. I remember thinking how out of place he looked in that 1940s kitchen, in his black T-shirt and jeans, the image of this boy I'd secretly fancied at my school. Right down to those beautiful dangerous eyes.

This is so unfair, I thought dreamily. They never told me the Opposition could be beautiful.

'We can take any form we like,' said the boy softly.

He snapped his fingers like a magician. Suddenly, shadowy little creatures were swarming everywhere, blindly bumping into each other, falling into the sink. The sound they made was out of my worst nightmares—a skittery insect sound which got right inside my head.

'I'm scared, Mum,' Molly moaned.

Her voice shook me out of my panic. Call yourself an angel, Melanie Beeby? I scolded myself. This is your basic good-versus-evil type situation. So just pull yourself together!

I stepped in front of the boy, holding out my divine insignia. I was shaking all over.

'Maybe I don't look much like an angel,' I quavered, 'but I'm here on official Agency business and Molly's under angelic protection. So don't even try to touch her.'

The boy laughed. 'Oh, but I haven't

come for Molly. I've come for you!'

I froze. Total brain melt, I thought. I am so stupid.

I'd made it so easy for them. Leaving my mates in the lurch. Deluding myself I was on a cosmic mission. I had this wonderful new life, I thought. And I threw it away. All for nothing.

'That's right,' said the boy. 'And by the time we've finished with you, that's exactly what you'll be. Nothing.'

He looked straight at me, and his beautiful eyes were totally empty.

'NOTHING,' he repeated.

Now I'm a girl who, if someone says I look pale, faints right on cue.

And I'm not proud of this, OK, but I immediately felt myself dissolving like a sugar cube. *It's happening*, I thought despairingly. I'm not a person. I'm not an angel. I'm no-one, I'm nothing. Soon I'll just be an empty space. It's all over . . .

Except, it wasn't.

'Erm, hang about!' I said suddenly. 'What am I meant to be scared of exactly? I've already lost everything I care about. I've got nothing left TO lose. Apart from wowing me with your naff special FX, there's not a thing you can do.' I drew myself up to my full height. 'So stop wasting my time, moron!'

He blew me a scornful kiss. 'Diddums. Like I actually care.'

But the Opposition's gruesome FX were already fading like a bad dream.

'There's the door,' I said in my snottiest voice. 'Mind it doesn't hit you in the backside on the way out.'

I turned my back as if he'd ceased to exist. And suddenly I could breathe again. He'd gone.

Given my record, I probably wasn't the best angel to save Molly, but I *was* the only angel available. So I touched my angel tags, and with a WHOOSH of cosmic energy, I willed myself to become visible.

There was a gasp from under the table.

I'd done it! I'd actually materialised! I was so thrilled with myself that my mind went a total blank. What shall I say? I panicked. Then vaguely familiar words floated into my head. I was only six when I played the angel in our school nativity, but it came back like yesterday. Well, kind of.

'Erm—fear not!' I said huskily. 'For lo! I am the angel Melanie and I have come to let you know you are not alone.'

Molly crawled out, her eyes filled with awe. Then I caught sight of my reflection in the hall and my eyes filled with awe too.

The mirror glowed with a rosy light. Inside the rosy halo was a wonderful being with wings, the kind a terrified child would instantly recognise as an angel.

My moment of weird glory lasted all of five seconds.

Then Molly's mum rushed in, her face absolutely white. 'Thank heaven!' she sobbed. She scooped Molly up in her arms and hurried out of the door.

'It's all right Mum,' I heard Molly gabble. 'I saw a beautiful angel and she said don't be frightened, so I wasn't.'

My knees went to jelly with pure relief. I closed my eyes and a silly smile spread slowly over my face. I don't think I've ever felt as happy as I did in that moment. I saved Molly all by myself, I thought. I really really did it.

Then an unearthly light burst upon my closed eyelids. When I opened them, Michael was standing there. He held out his hand for my angel tags.

'I'll have those, thanks,' he said coldly.

CHAPTER TEN

I'd tried every trick I knew to get myself to sleep. I'd had a long bath by candlelight. I'd helped myself to Lola's stash of twenty-second-century drinking chocolate. I'd even listened to my favourite late-night music turned way down low.

I'd tried everything and I was still as jumpy as a Mexican bean. In normal circumstances I'd have died of fright. But angels can't die. Not even angel failures like me.

Typically I never did get around to reading that Handbook, so I had no idea what we did instead. I just hoped it wasn't like that depressing fairytale, where the little mermaid turns into sea foam.

I switched off the light and got into bed. But the dark didn't make me sleepy, just lonely. I padded over to the window and gazed out over the beautiful, beautiful city. Its lights sparkled like millions of fallen stars.

My eyes prickled and blurred. Don't think, Melanie. Don't think about that wraparound sky so blue that you can't tell where it leaves off and the sea begins. Don't think about Lola and Reuben, or that sweet-faced boy Orlando. You had a once-in-eternity opportunity and you blew it.

When I first got here, I used to imagine how gobsmacked Miss Rowntree would be if she ever learned that her most troublesome pupil had been picked for angel school. I was constantly dreaming up dramatic situations where I zoomed back to Earth and wowed my old teacher with my amazing skills. 'Melanie,' she'd gasp. 'I'm truly sorry I misunderstood you. You had hidden depths, which I completely failed to see.'

But now it seemed I hadn't changed

 133

after all—just gone round in one big dreary circle.

After I was brought back in disgrace, Michael quietly listed every one of my misdemeanours. Abandoning the other members of my team, thus putting them at risk; materialising to a human child without permission; claiming to be on Agency business when actually it was all my own stupid idea . . .

I'd broken so many celestial rules, it was probably some kind of record. I couldn't blame the Academy for wanting to throw me out.

'It's out of my hands,' Michael had said quietly. 'The Academy Council will deal with you in due course. Until then you will not be permitted to leave the school grounds.'

And he'd looked so disappointed, I'd have given anything to be human again so I could just crawl off and die.

Yet I didn't regret what I'd done. Once I had that moment of clarity in the tube station, I had to do what I believed was right. Even though it turned out to be totally, totally wrong.

It's like, up until that moment I'd

134

just been playing a beautiful magical game called Angel. But the instant I walked away, that was when it became the real thing.

I hadn't set eyes on my mates since I got back. Our entire class had gone off on an end-of-term jaunt to some exotic wildlife park. The dorm was totally dead, and I preferred it that way.

I just couldn't face them after what happened. By the time they came back, it would all be over. I'd be sea foam, or whatever.

I caught sight of my stricken face in the mirror. 'We were meant to be the three cosmic musketeers,' I whispered.

Now I'd never go time-travelling with my friends, or learn to send dreams like Orlando.

'Stop torturing yourself, Mel,' I said aloud. 'Try to get through the night with a bit of dignity, OK?'

I'd been summoned to appear before the Council early next morning. But I was so nervous I got there way ahead of time.

'I don't think they're quite ready for you, Melanie,' said the school secretary, avoiding my eyes. 'Perhaps you'd care to take a seat.'

I could tell she despised me. But I was too numb to care. Get used to it, Mel, I thought drearily. In ten minutes you'll be a fallen angel. The lowest of the low.

The chamber door had gorgeous stained-glass panels. I sat staring at it for so long, I could have drawn it from memory. From time to time I heard raised voices. There was a major debate going on. I caught glimpses of swirling robes as various archangels swept past.

I'd never met any archangels, apart from Michael. But Lola once told me they made space aliens seem almost cuddly.

I felt utterly alone. Desperate for comfort, I reached for my angel insignia to reassure myself, but my hand closed around air.

Then I seemed to hear Lola's voice. 'What are you doing, Boo?' she demanded. 'Sitting here like a total turkey while these terrifying beings decide what to do with you. DO something, girl!'

'Yeah, Mel,' Reuben teased. 'Put your Houdini powers into reverse and stay put for a change!'

It was like my best friends were actually with me in the waiting room!

'OK,' I whispered. 'I will.'

And I stood up, tugged down my skirt and knocked on the door.

There was no answer, so I took a deep breath and went in.

With so many archangels in one room, the light levels were truly awesome. Michael was there, to my relief. And from what I remembered of our angelic history lessons, I guessed I was also looking at Gabriel, Raphael, Uriel, Jophiel and Chamuel. Just don't ask me which terrifying face belonged to which archangel.

The archangels stared back, appalled. I willed my jelly knees to hold me up.

'I don't mean to be disrespectful,' I croaked. 'But you've got to let me stay. You've just got to.'

The secretary rushed in. 'I am so sorry,' she panted. 'I distinctly told

Miss Beeby to wait outside.'

'That's quite all right,' said a remote voice. 'We're most interested to hear what she has to say for herself.'

I closed my eyes. 'Um,' I said. 'First, I want to let you know, that I do realise I really messed up badly.'

'Hardly a controversial insight,' said an identically distant voice.

'I know that,' I said humbly. 'But you truly can't imagine how sorry I am. I've learned a lot since I've been here.'

One of the archangels gave a weary sigh.

'It's the truth,' I said quickly. 'Mr Allbright is a great teacher and my friends helped heaps, and I think that one day I could shape up to be a really wicked trouble-shooter. Brilliant trouble-shooter, I mean,' I corrected hastily.

'Melanie,' Michael began. 'I don't think this is—'

I rushed on desperately. 'I let my team mates down and that was wrong. But that doesn't mean you guys were wrong when you picked me to be an angel.' My voice cracked with misery.

138

'If you'll just give me a second chance,' I pleaded huskily, 'I'll never let you down again. I'll work night and day. I'll even read my—'

An irritable voice interrupted me. 'Enough! This is extremely touching, my dear, but I'm afraid you left it too late. We came to our verdict a few minutes before you burst in. And as you know, the Council's decision is final.'

I felt a total fool. 'Oh,' I said. 'I'm—I didn't . . .'

I was suddenly blinded with tears. I was done for. My angelic career had finally crashed and burned. I blundered towards the door.

'Melanie?' said Michael softly. 'Don't you want to know what that verdict was?'

I turned in despair. 'I suppose, that sinister sea foam thing,' I whispered.

'Sea foam?' said Uriel, or possibly Jophiel, looking utterly baffled.

Michael took charge. 'Melanie, the Council unanimously agreed that you may stay,' he said.

I could feel a leftover tear tracking

 139

down my chin. 'Stay?' I echoed blankly.

It's a dream, I thought. I'll wake up in a minute and I'll have to go to the *real* Academy Council.

'You did remarkably well in your exams, Melanie,' said Michael. 'In fact you got a distinction.'

I think it was Michael's smile that made me know I wasn't dreaming. I felt it right inside my heart. Suddenly I heard what he'd said.

'A distinction!' I shrieked. 'Totally luminous!'

'You also lost your team a much-deserved HALO award,' Gabriel or Chamuel pointed out.

'Oh,' I said, ashamed. 'I didn't know.'

'And your angelic presentation skills still need a little work,' he added sternly. 'I quote: "For lo! I am the angel Melanie", etcetera etcetera.'

My face burned. There are SO not any secrets in Heaven!

Then Uriel—it was definitely Uriel —said something so beautiful, I just know I'll remember it for ever.

'However,' he said gently, 'a trouble-

shooting angel, far from Heaven, must sometimes improvise. And your heart, as humans say, was very much in the right place.'

CHAPTER ELEVEN

The morning of the end-of-term party, Lola and I went on a major shopping spree.

'So what was he like?' Lola said, holding up a sugary pink baby-doll dress patterned with little love hearts.

'Yuk!' I said. 'Nightmare.'

'He was yuk?'

'The dress, dumbo. The Opposition guy was in a totally different category of nightmare. Did you still have horror films in your time?'

Lola shuddered. 'My brothers loved those things. Me, I couldn't see the point. All those gruesome special FX.'

'*That's* the category,' I said. 'The spooky thing was, he looked exactly like this boy I fancied at school.'

Lola giggled. 'A really *bad* boy, I bet.'

We went back to hunting along the rails.

'Boo, do you even know what you're looking for?' Lola sighed.

I showed her a scarlet leather catsuit. 'What do you think?'

'Miaow!' grinned Lola. 'Maybe you should go for something more discreet!'

And she picked out a Clark Kent-type suit. We went into fits of giggles.

'Ooh, yes! All I need is those sexy black-rimmed spectacles,' I told her.

'OK,' said Lola. 'We've got exactly one hour to get this perfect look together. Then we've got to do some serious cooking for the party.'

I remembered something. 'Lollie, did you and Reuben like, transmit good vibes to me or something, when I was in with the big guys?'

Lola suddenly looked vague. 'Maybe. I don't remember.'

'Sure you don't.' I gave her a hug. 'Thanks. I got them.'

Exactly one hour later I had the

perfect trouble-shooting outfit—cropped top, combats and some cool boots. To me that look says committed, it says *now*, it says ready for action. I mean, I'm an angel, so I should look totally divine, right?

We held our class party down on the beach. Everything was so lovely, I kept thinking it couldn't possibly get any lovelier—but each time the party morphed effortlessly into a whole new phase.

At one point I found myself standing beside Flora. 'Sorry about losing you guys that award,' I mumbled. I thought she'd be furious, but she just gave a cool little shrug.

'There's always next term.'

People can SO surprise you. Take Amber for instance. It turns out she doesn't play the harp at all. Would you believe, bongo drums?!

Incidentally, Reuben aced his Earth Skills paper. Trust me, until you've seen a happy angel-angel, you do not know what happiness is!

Lola and I had the most fun teaching Reuben terrestrial-type DJing. In no time he'd developed his own style, mixing earthly and heavenly sounds and rhythms like you would NOT believe.

'Ya-ay! DJ Sweet Pea is in the house!' yelled Lola.

Then suddenly my bare arms were covered with goosebumps. Someone was calling me and I had to go.

I slipped down to the seashore, and there was Michael, waiting. He didn't speak, just picked up a beautiful shell from the water's edge and, with the sweetest smile, put it into my hand.

I held it for a moment, just to feel its smooth curved shape. Impulsively I put it to my ear. And then it happened, just like Lola said.

'Helix,' whispered the waves.

'It's my name,' I breathed. 'My true angel name.'